Mr. Carteret

David Gray

Alpha Editions

This edition published in 2023

ISBN : 9789357954051

Design and Setting By
Alpha Editions
www.alphaedis.com
Email - info@alphaedis.com

Contents

I
MR. CARTERET AND HIS FELLOW AMERICANS ABROAD

"It must have been highly interesting," observed Mrs. Archie Brawle; "so much pleasanter than a concert."

"Rather!" replied Lord Frederic. "It was ripping!"

Mrs. Ascott-Smith turned to Mr. Carteret. She had been listening to Lord Frederic Westcote, who had just come down from town where he had seen the Wild West show. "Is it so?" she asked. "Have you ever seen them?" By "them" she meant the Indians.

Mr. Carteret nodded.

"It seems so odd," continued Mrs. Archie Brawle, "that they should ride without saddles. Is it a pose?"

"No, I fancy not," replied Lord Frederic.

"They must get very tired without stirrups," insisted Mrs. Archie. "But perhaps they never ride very long at a time."

"That is possible," said Lord Frederic doubtfully. "They are only on about twenty minutes in the show."

Mr. Pringle, the curate, who had happened in to pay his monthly call upon Mrs. Ascott-Smith, took advantage of the pause. "Of course, I am no horseman," he began apprehensively, "and I have never seen the red Indians, either in their native wilds or in a show, but I have read not a little about them, and I have gathered that they almost live on horseback."

Major Hammerslea reached toward the tea table for another muffin and hemmed. "It is a very different thing," he said with heavy impressiveness. "It is a very different thing."

The curate looked expectant, as if believing that his remarks were going to be noticed. But nothing was farther from the Major's mind.

"What is so very different?" inquired Mrs. Ascott-Smith, after a pause had made it clear that the Major had ignored Pringle.

"It is one thing, my dear Madame, to ride a stunted, half-starved pony, as you say, 'bareback,' and another thing to ride a conditioned British hunter (he pronounced it huntaw) without a saddle. I must say that the latter is an impossibility." The oracle came to an end and the material Major began on the muffin.

There was an approving murmur of assent. The Major was the author of "Schooling and Riding British Hunters"; however, it was not only his authority which swayed the company, but individual conviction. Of the dozen people in the room, excepting Pringle, all rode to hounds with more or less enthusiasm, and no one had ever seen any one hunting without a saddle and no one had ever experienced any desire to try the experiment. Obviously it was an absurdity.

"Nevertheless," observed Lord Frederic, "I must say their riding was very creditable—quite as good as one sees on any polo field in England."

Major Hammerslea looked at him severely, as if his youth were not wholly an excuse. "It is, as I said," he observed. "It is one thing to ride an American pony and another to ride a British hunter. One requires horsemanship, the other does not. And horsemanship," he continued, "which properly is the guiding of a horse across country, requires years of study and experience."

Lord Frederic looked somewhat unconvinced but he said nothing.

"Of course the dear Major (she called it deah Majaw) is unquestionably right," said Mrs. Ascott-Smith.

"Undoubtedly," said Mr. Carteret. "I suppose that he has often seen Indians ride?"

"Have you often seen these Indians ride?" inquired Mrs. Ascott-Smith of the Major.

"Do you mean Indians or the Red Men of North America?" replied the Major. "And do you mean upon ponies in a show or upon British hunters?"

"Which do you mean?" asked Mrs. Ascott-Smith.

"I suppose that I mean American Indians," said Mr. Carteret, "and either upon ponies or upon British hunters."

"No," said the Major, "I have not. Have you?"

"Not upon British hunters," said Mr. Carteret.

"But do you think that they could?" inquired Lord Frederic.

"It would be foolish of me to express an opinion," replied Mr. Carteret, "because, in the first place, I have never seen them ride British hunters over fences—"

"They would come off at the first obstacle," observed the Major, more in sorrow than in anger.

"And in the second place," continued Mr. Carteret, "I am perhaps naturally prejudiced in behalf of my fellow countrymen."

Mrs. Ascott-Smith looked at him anxiously. His sister had married a British peer. "But you Americans are quite distinct from the red Indians," she said. "We quite understand that nowadays. To be sure, my dear Aunt—" She stopped.

"Rather!" said Mrs. Archie Brawle. "You don't even intermarry with them, do you?"

"That is a matter of personal taste," said Mr. Carteret. "There is no law against it."

"But nobody that one knows—" began Mrs. Ascott-Smith.

"There was John Rolfe," said Mr. Carteret; "he was a very well known chap."

"Do you know him?" asked Mrs. Brawle.

The curate sniggered. His hour of triumph had come. "Rolfe is dead," he said.

"Really!" said Mrs. Brawle, coldly. "It had quite slipped my mind. You see I never read the papers during the hunting. But is his wife received?"

"I believe that she was," said Mr. Carteret.

The curate was still sniggering and Mrs. Brawle put her glass in her eye and looked at him. Then she turned to Mr. Carteret. "But all this," she said, "of course, has nothing to do with the question. Do you think that these red Indians could ride bareback across our country?"

"As I said before," replied Mr. Carteret, "it would be silly of me to express an opinion, but I should be interested in seeing them try it."

"I have a topping idea!" cried Lord Frederic. He was an enthusiastic, simple-minded fellow.

"You must tell us," exclaimed Mrs. Ascott-Smith.

"Let us have them down, and take them hunting!"

"How exciting!" exclaimed Mrs. Ascott-Smith. "What sport!"

The Major looked at her reprovingly. "It would be as I said," he observed.

"But it would be rather interesting," said Mrs. Brawle.

"It might," said the Major, "it might be interesting."

"It would be ripping!" said Lord Frederic. "But how can we manage it?"

"I'll mount them," said the Major with a grim smile. "My word! They shall have the pick of my stable though I have to spend a month rebreaking horses that have run away."

"But it isn't the difficulty of mounting them," said Lord Frederic. "You see I've never met any of these chaps." He turned to Mr. Carteret with a sudden inspiration. "Are any of them friends of yours?" he asked.

Mrs. Ascott-Smith looked anxiously at Mr. Carteret, as if she feared that it would develop that some of the people in the show were his cousins.

"No," he replied, "I don't think so, although I may have met some of them in crossing the reservations. But I once went shooting with Grady, one of the managers of the show."

"Better yet!" said Lord Frederic. "Do you think that he would come and bring some of them down?" he asked.

"I think he would," said Mr. Carteret. He knew that the showman was strong in Grady—as well as the sportsman.

The Major rose to go to the billiard room. "I have one piece of advice to give you," he said. "This prank is harmless enough, but establish a definite understanding with this fellow that you are not to be liable in damages for personal injuries which his Indians may receive. Explain to him that it is not child's play and have him put it in writing."

"You mean to have him execute a kind of release?" said Mr. Carteret.

"Precisely that," said the Major. "I was once sued for twenty pounds by a groom that fell off my best horse and let him run away, and damme, the fellow recovered." He bowed to the ladies and left the room.

"Of course we can fix all that up," said Lord Frederic. "The old chap is a bit overcautious nowadays, but how can we get hold of this fellow Grady?"

"I'll wire him at once, if you wish," said Mr. Carteret, and he went to the writing table. "When do you want him to come down?" he asked, as he began to write.

"We might take them out with the Quorn on Saturday," said Lord Frederic, "but the meet is rather far for us. Perhaps it would be better to have them on Thursday with Charley Ploversdale's hounds."

Mr. Carteret hesitated a moment. "Wouldn't Ploversdale be apt to be fussy about experiments? He's rather conservative, you know, about the way people are turned out. I saw him send a man home one day who was out without a hat. It was an American who was afraid that hats made his hair come out."

"Pish," said Lord Frederic, "Charley Ploversdale is mild as a dove."

"Suit yourself," said Mr. Carteret. "I'll make it Thursday. One more question," he added. "How many shall I ask him to bring down?" At this moment the Major came into the room again. He had mislaid his eyeglasses.

"I should think that a dozen would be about the right number," said Lord Frederic, replying to Mr. Carteret. "It would be very imposing."

"Too many!" said the Major. "We must mount them on good horses and I don't want my entire stable ruined by men who have never lepped a fence."

"I think the Major is right about the matter of numbers," said Mr. Carteret. "How would three do?"

"Make it three," said the Major.

Before dinner was over a reply came from Grady saying that he and three bucks would be pleased to arrive Thursday morning prepared for a hunting party.

This took place on Monday, and at various times during Tuesday and Wednesday Mr. Carteret gave the subject thought. By Thursday morning his views had ripened. He ordered his tea and eggs to be served in his room and came down a little past ten dressed in knickerbockers and an old shooting coat. He wandered into the dining-room and found Mrs. Ascott-Smith sitting by the fire entertaining Lord Frederic, as he went to and from the sideboard in search of things to eat.

"Good morning," said Mr. Carteret, hoarsely.

Lord Frederic looked around and as he noticed Mr. Carteret's clothes his face showed surprise.

"Hello!" he said, "you had better hurry and change, or you will be late. We have to start in half an hour to meet Grady."

Mr. Carteret coughed. "I don't think that I can go out to-day. It is a great disappointment."

"Not going hunting?" exclaimed Mrs. Ascott-Smith. "What is the matter?"

"I have a bad cold," said Mr. Carteret miserably.

"But, my dear fellow," exclaimed Lord Frederic, "it will do your cold a world of good!"

"Not a cold like mine," said Mr. Carteret.

"But this is the day, don't you know?" said Lord Frederic. "How am I going to manage things without you?"

"All that you have to do is to meet them at the station and take them to the meet," said Mr. Carteret. "Everything else has been arranged."

"But I'm awfully disappointed," said Lord Frederic. "I had counted on you to help, don't you see, and introduce them to Ploversdale. It would be more graceful for an American to do it than for me. You understand?"

"Yes," said Mr. Carteret, "I understand. It's a great disappointment, but I must bear it philosophically."

Mrs. Ascott-Smith looked at him sympathetically, and he coughed twice. "You are suffering," she said. "Freddy, you really must not urge him to expose himself. Have you a pain here?" she inquired, touching herself in the region of the pleura.

"Yes," said Mr. Carteret, "it is just there, but I daresay that it will soon be better."

"I am afraid not," said his hostess. "This is the way pneumonia begins. You must take a medicine that I have. They say that it is quite wonderful for inflammatory colds. I'll send Hodgson for it," and she touched the bell.

"Please, please don't take that trouble," entreated Mr. Carteret.

"But you must take it," said Mrs. Ascott-Smith. "They call it Broncholine. You pour it in a tin and inhale it or swallow it, I forget which, but it's very efficacious. They used it on Teddy's pony when it was sick. The little creature died, but that was because they gave it too much, or not enough, I forget which."

Hodgson appeared and Mrs. Ascott-Smith gave directions about the Broncholine.

"I thank you very much," said Mr. Carteret humbly. "I'll go to my room and try it at once."

"That's a good chap!" said Lord Frederic, "perhaps you will feel so much better that you can join us."

"Perhaps," said Mr. Carteret gloomily, "or it may work as it did on the pony." And he left the room.

After Hodgson had departed from his chamber leaving explicit directions as to how and how not to use the excellent Broncholine, Mr. Carteret poured a quantity of it from the bottle and threw it out of the window, resolving to be on the safe side. Then he looked at his boots and his pink coat and white leathers, which were laid out upon the bed. "I don't think there can be any danger," he thought, "if I turn up after they have started. I loathe stopping in all day." He dressed leisurely, ordered his second horse to be sent on, and some time after the rest of the household had gone to the meet he sallied forth. As he knew the country and the coverts which Lord Ploversdale would draw, he counted on joining the tail of the hunt, thus keeping out of sight. He inquired of a rustic if he had seen hounds pass and receiving "no" for an answer, he jogged on at a faster trot, fearing that the hunt might have gone away in some other direction.

As he came around a bend in the road, he saw four women riding toward him, and as they drew near, he saw that they were Lady Violet Weatherbone and her three daughters. These young ladies were known as the Three Guardsmen, a sobriquet not wholly inappropriate; for, as Lord Frederic described them, they were "big-boned, upstanding fillies," between twenty-five and thirty and very hard goers across any country, and always together.

"Good morning," said Mr. Carteret, bowing. "I suppose the hounds are close by?" It was a natural assumption, as Lady Violet on hunting days was never very far from the hounds.

"I do not know," she responded, and her tone further implied that she did not care.

Mr. Carteret hesitated a moment. "Is anything the matter?" he asked. "Has anything happened?"

"Yes," said Lady Violet frankly, "something has happened." Here the daughters modestly turned their horses away.

"Some one," continued Lady Violet, "brought savages to the meet." She paused impressively.

"Not really!" said Mr. Carteret. It was all that he could think of to say.

"Yes," said Lady Violet, "and while it would have mattered little to me, it was impossible—" She motioned with her head toward the three maidens, and paused.

"Forgive me," said Mr. Carteret, "but do I quite understand?"

"At the first I thought," said Lady Violet, "that they were attired in painted fleshings, but upon using my glass, it was clear that I was mistaken. Otherwise, I should have brought them away at the first moment."

"I see," said Mr. Carteret. "It is most unfortunate!"

"It is, indeed!" said Lady Violet; "but the matter will not be allowed to drop. They were brought to the meet by that young profligate, Lord Frederic Westcote."

"You amaze me," said Mr. Carteret. He bowed, started his horse, and jogged along for five minutes, then he turned to the right upon a crossroad and suddenly found himself with hounds. They were feathering excitedly about the mouth of a tile drain into which the fox had evidently gone. No master, huntsmen or whips were in sight, but sitting wet and mud-daubed upon horses dripping with muddy water were Grady dressed in cowboy costume and three naked Indians. Mr. Carteret glanced about over the country and understood. They had swum the brook at the place where it ran between steep clay banks and the rest of the field had gone around to the bridge. As he looked toward the south, he saw Lord Ploversdale riding furiously toward him followed by Smith, the huntsman. Grady had not recognized Mr. Carteret turned out in pink as he was, and for the moment the latter decided to remain incognito.

Before Lord Ploversdale, Master of Fox-hounds, reached the road, he began waving his whip. He appeared excited. "What do you mean by riding upon my hounds?" he shouted. He said this in several ways with various accompanying phrases, but neither the Indians nor Grady seemed to notice him. It occurred to Mr. Carteret that, although Lord Ploversdale's power of expression was wonderful for England, it nevertheless fell short of Arizona standards. Then, however, he noticed that Grady was absorbed in adjusting a kodak camera, with which he was evidently about to take a picture of the Indians alone with the hounds. He drew back in order both to avoid being in the field of the picture and to avoid too close proximity with Lord Ploversdale as he came over the fence into the road.

"What do you mean, sir!" shouted the enraged Master of Fox-hounds, as he pulled up his horse.

"A little more in the middle," replied Grady, still absorbed in taking the picture.

"A little more in the middle"

Lord Ploversdale hesitated. He was speechless with surprise for the moment.

Grady pressed the button and began putting up the machine.

"What do you mean by riding on my hounds, you and these persons?" demanded Lord Ploversdale.

"We didn't," said Grady amicably, "but if your bunch of dogs don't know enough to keep out of the way of a horse, they ought to learn."

Lord Ploversdale looked aghast and Smith, the huntsman, pinched himself to make sure that he was not dreaming.

"Many thanks for your advice," said Lord Ploversdale. "May I inquire who you and your friends may be?"

"I'm James Grady," said that gentleman. "This," he said, pointing to the Indian nearest, "is Chief Hole-in-the-Ground of the Olgallala Sioux. Him in the middle is Mr. Jim Snake, and the one beyond is Chief Skytail, a Pawnee."

"Thank you, that is very interesting," said Lord Ploversdale, with polite irony. "Now will you kindly take them home?"

"See here," said Grady, strapping the camera to his saddle, "I was invited to this hunt, regular, and if you hand me out any more hostile talk—" He paused.

"Who invited you?" inquired Lord Ploversdale.

"One of your own bunch," said Grady, "Lord Frederic Westcote. I'm no butterin."

"Your language is difficult to understand," said Lord Ploversdale. "Where is Lord Frederic Westcote?"

Mr. Carteret had watched the field approaching as fast as whip and spur could drive them, and in the first flight he noticed Lord Frederic and the Major. For this reason he still hesitated about thrusting himself into the discussion. It seemed that the interference of a third party could only complicate matters, inasmuch as Lord Frederic would so soon be upon the spot.

Lord Ploversdale looked across the field impatiently. "I've no doubt, my good fellow, that Lord Frederic Westcote brought you here and I'll see him about it, but kindly take these fellows home. They'll kill all my hounds."

"Now you're beginning to talk reasonable," said Grady. "I'll discuss with you."

The words were hardly out of his mouth before hounds gave tongue riotously and went off. The fox had slipped out of the other end of the drain and old Archer had found the line.

As if shot out of a gun the three Indians dashed at the stake-and-bound fence on the farther side of the road, joyously using their heavy quirts on the Major's thoroughbreds. Skytail's horse being hurried too much, blundered his take-off, hit above the knees and rolled over on the Chief who was sitting tight. There was a stifled grunt and then the Pawnee word "Go-dam!"

Hole-in-the-Ground looked back and laughed one of the few laughs of his life. It was a joke which he could understand. Then he used the quirt again to make the most of his advantage.

"That one is finished," said Lord Ploversdale gratefully. But as the words were in his mouth, Skytail rose with his horse, vaulted up and was away.

The M. F. H. followed over the fence shouting at Smith to whip off the hounds. But the hounds were going too fast. They had got a view of the fox and three whooping horsemen were behind them driving them on.

The first flight of the field followed the M. F. H. out of the road and so did Mr. Carteret, and presently he found himself riding between Lord Frederic and the Major. They were both a bit winded and had evidently come fast.

"I say," exclaimed Lord Frederic, "where did you come from?"

"I was cured by the Broncholine," said Mr. Carteret, "amazing stuff!"

"Is your horse fresh?" asked Lord Frederic.

"Yes," replied Mr. Carteret, "I happened upon them at the road."

"Then go after that man Grady," said Lord Frederic, "and implore him to take those beggars home. They have been riding on hounds for twenty minutes."

"Were they able," asked Mr. Carteret, "to stay with their horses at the fences?"

"Stay with their horses!" puffed the Major.

"Go on like a good chap," said Lord Frederic, "stop that fellow or I shall be expelled from the hunt; perhaps put in jail. Was Ploversdale vexed?" he added.

"I should judge by his language," said Mr. Carteret, "that he was vexed."

"Hurry on," said Lord Frederic. "Put your spurs in."

Mr. Carteret gave his horse its head and he shot to the front, but Grady was nearly a field in the lead and it promised to be a long chase as he was on the Major's black thoroughbred. The cowboy rode along with a loose rein and an easy balance seat. At his fences he swung his hat and cheered. He seemed to be enjoying himself and Mr. Carteret was anxious lest he might begin to shoot for pure delight. Such a demonstration would have been misconstrued. Nearly two hundred yards ahead at the heels of the pack galloped the Indians, and in the middle distance between them and Grady rode Lord Ploversdale and Smith vainly trying to overtake the hounds and whip them off. Behind and trailing over a mile or more came the field and the rest of the hunt servants in little groups, all awestruck at what had happened. It was unspeakable that Lord Ploversdale's hounds which had been hunted by his father and his grandfather should be so scandalized.

Mr. Carteret finally got within a length of Grady and hailed him.

"Hello, Carty," said Grady, "glad to see you. I thought you were sick. What can I do? They've stampeded. But it's a great ad. for the show, isn't it? I've got four reporters in a hack on the road."

"Forget about the show," said Mr. Carteret. "This isn't any laughing matter. Ploversdale's hounds are one of the smartest packs in England. You don't understand."

"It will make all the better story in the papers," said Grady.

"No, it won't," said Mr. Carteret. "They won't print it. It's like a blasphemy upon the Church."

"Whoop!" yelled Grady, as they tore through a bullfinch.

"Call them off," said Mr. Carteret, straightening his hat.

"But I can't catch 'em," said Grady, and that was the truth.

Lord Ploversdale, however, had been gaining on the Indians, and by the way in which he clubbed his heavy crop, loaded at the butt, it was apparent that he meant to put an end to the proceedings if he could.

Just then hounds swept over the crest of a green hill and as they went down the other side, they viewed the fox in the field beyond. He was in distress, and it looked as if the pack would kill in the open. They were running wonderfully together, the traditional blanket would have covered them, and in the natural glow of pride which came over the M. F. H., he loosened his grip upon the crop. But as the hounds viewed the fox so did the three sons of the wilderness who were following close behind. From the hilltop fifty of the hardest going men in England saw Hole-in-the-Ground flogging his horse with the heavy quirt which hung from his wrist. The outraged British hunter shot forward scattering hounds to right and left, flew a ditch and hedge and was close on the fox who had stopped to make a last stand. Without drawing rein, the astonished onlookers saw the lean Indian suddenly disappear under the neck of his horse and almost instantly swing back into his seat waving a brown thing above his head. *Hole-in-the-Ground had caught the fox!*

"Most unprecedented!" Mr. Carteret heard the Major exclaim. He pulled up his horse, as the field did theirs, and waited apprehensively. He saw Hole-in-the-Ground circle around, jerk the Major's five hundred guinea hunter to a standstill close to Lord Ploversdale and address him. He was speaking in his own language.

As the Chief went on, he saw Grady smile.

"He says," said Grady translating, "that the white chief can eat the fox if he wants him. He's proud himself bein' packed with store grub."

The English onlookers heard and beheld with blank faces. It was beyond them.

The M. F. H. bowed stiffly as Hole-in-the-Ground's offer was made known to him. He regarded them a moment in thought. A vague light was breaking in upon him. "Aw, thank you," he said, "thanks awfully. Smith, take the fox. Good afternoon!"

Then he wheeled his horse, called the hounds in with his horn and trotted out to the road that led to the kennels. Lord Ploversdale, though he had never been out of England, was cast in a large mold.

The three Indians sat on their panting horses, motionless, stolidly facing the curious gaze of the crowd; or rather they looked through the crowd, as the lion with the high breeding of the desert looks through and beyond the faces that stare and gape before the bars of his cage.

"Most amazing! Most amazing!" muttered the Major.

"It is," said Mr. Carteret, "if you have never been away from this." He made a sweeping gesture over the restricted English scenery, pampered and brought up by hand.

"Been away from this?" repeated the Major. "I don't understand."

Mr. Carteret turned to him. How could he explain it?

"With us," he began, laying an emphasis on the "us." Then he stopped. "Look into their eyes," he said hopelessly.

The Major looked at him blankly. How could he, Major Hammerslea of "The Blues," tell what those inexplicable dark eyes saw beyond the fenced tillage! What did he know of the brown, bare, illimitable range under the noonday sun, the evening light on far, silent mountains, the starlit desert!

II
HOW MR. CARTERET PROPOSED

Barclay slowly guided his horse through the mounted throng to the spot where Mr. Carteret was sitting on a chestnut thoroughbred horse watching hounds as they came straggling out of the spinney. They had drawn blank. The fox was not at home. When Barclay reached his friend he pulled up casually as if he had come for no express purpose, and said nothing. After a few moments he began, as if an idea had just come to him:

"It has occurred to me, Carty," he said, "that if we brought American horses to England, we could make a lot of money."

"That idea has occurred to others," replied Mr. Carteret, without turning his head. He was absorbed in the enjoyable discovery that the scene before him was like a hunting-print. The browns of the wood and bracken, the winter green of the hill pastures, the scarlet coats, the gray sky of the English winter, were all happily true to art. "As I say," he went on, "the idea has occurred to others, but I have never heard that any one made money."

"That is because they haven't sent over good horses," said Barclay. "Suppose we brought over only such thoroughbred horses as we raise on the Wyoming ranch."

"I don't think it would make any difference," said Mr. Carteret. "There is a prejudice against American horses."

"Exactly," said Barclay; "and the way to meet it would be to have them ridden and handled by a well-known Englishman. In fact, I have the man in mind."

"Who?"

"Young Granvil," was the answer.

Why Barclay should be interested in making money out of a horse business or in any other way had perplexed Mr. Carteret, for it was not according to his habits of mind. Now it became clear to him, and he suppressed a cynical smile. "I don't suppose Lady Withers has discussed this matter with you," he observed.

"In a general way, yes," replied Barclay; "but it was my suggestion."

"Of course," said Mr. Carteret.

Barclay paused awkwardly for a moment, then he said: "Why shouldn't I talk it over with Lady Withers? She is a very intelligent woman, and a good judge of a horse."

"An excellent judge of almost everything," said his friend, "and especially of young men. My son," he continued (Barclay was five years his junior), "it is commendable of Lady Withers to provide for the Hon. Cecil James Montague Granvil. He is her nephew and flat broke, and he needs people to look after him because he is almost less than half-witted. But that is no reason why you should be the person to look after him."

"You are unjust to Cecil," said Barclay, "and most unkind in your insinuations as to Lady Withers. This was my own idea entirely, and I think it would be profitable for both of us. You know you are always complaining because I don't take more interest in the ranches."

"If I have been unkind to Lady Withers," said Mr. Carteret, "I am going to be much more so."

Barclay looked challengingly. "What do you mean?" he demanded.

"Lady Withers," said Mr. Carteret, "is a widow, aged forty-four,—you can verify that in Burke,—a man-eater by temperament and habit. You are twelve years younger than she, with a great deal more money than is good for you. Whether she intends to marry you I don't pretend to know, but it is not unlikely. At any rate, you are unquestionably on the list as a source of income and supply."

Somewhat to Mr. Carteret's surprise, Barclay listened calmly.

"Do you really think Lady Withers considers me eligible?" he asked.

"She does, if she has any true conception of your securities."

Barclay smiled a pleased smile. "I shall not stop to discuss Lady Withers's age," he said. "Have you any objections to her aside from that?"

Mr. Carteret looked at him with outward calm, but inwardly he was filled with horror. "Are you engaged to her?" he asked.

"I am not," said Barclay.

"Then I shall tell you," he went on, "that I have objections. Their nature I have no time to disclose at present further than to say that any woman who puts a nice girl like her niece upon the horse she is riding to-day is a bad lot."

Barclay's expression changed. "What is the matter with the horse?" he demanded.

"I'm not sure that I know *all* that is the matter with him," said Carty, "but I wouldn't ride him over a fence for the Bank of England."

"Do you know that, or are you just talking?" said Barclay.

"I ought to know," said the other. "I owned him. After what he did to me, I ought to have shot him. We'd better jog along," he added, "or we shall get pocketed and never get through the gate."

The huntsman had called his hounds and was carrying them to the next cover, and Mr. Carteret set his horse to a trot and struggled for a place in the vast scarlet-coated throng that surged toward the gate leading out of the meadow. At the same time Barclay disappeared.

The vast scarlet-coated throng that surged toward the gate

"I hope he tells Lady Withers about the horse," said Mr. Carteret to himself. "If she doesn't keep her hands off him, I shall tell her several things myself."

Just at that moment the eddying currents of the human maelstrom brought him alongside a slender little figure in a weather-beaten habit and a bowler hat jammed down to her ears over a mass of golden hair. Although the knot of hair was twisted cruelly tight, and although the hat did its best to cover it, even a man's eye could see that it was profuse and wonderful. It was unnecessary for him to look at the horse. He knew that he was beside Lady Mary Granvil, Lady Withers's niece. "Good afternoon," he said and she turned toward him. It was a sad rather than a pretty face, but one's attention never rested long upon it, for a pair of gray eyes shone from under the brows, and after the first glance one looked at the eyes.

"Good afternoon," he said again. The eyes rather disconcerted him. "Do you happen to know anything about that horse you're riding?"

"It's one that my aunt bought quite recently," said the girl. "She and Cecil wished me to try it."

"I hope you won't think me rude," said Mr. Carteret, "but I once owned him, and I think you'll find this horse of mine a much pleasanter beast to ride. I'll have the saddles changed."

Lady Mary looked at him, and a light flashed in her gray eyes. "You are very good," she said, "but this is my aunt's horse, and my brother told me to ride it." She forged ahead, and disappeared in the currents of the crowd.

"I did that very badly," Mr. Carteret said to himself, and fell into the line and waited for his turn at the gate.

He and Barclay, Lady Withers, and many other people were stopping the week-end at Mrs. Ascott-Smith's, who had Chilliecote Abbey, and when he got home that afternoon he went at once to the great library, where the ceremony of tea was celebrated. The daylight was fading from the mullioned windows as it had faded on winter afternoons for three hundred years. Candles burned on the vacant card-tables, while the occupants of the room gathered in the glow of the great Elizabethan fireplace and conversed and ate. As he approached the circle, Lady Withers put down her tea cup.

"Did you have another run after we pulled out?" she asked.

"Yes," said Mr. Carteret; "rather a good one."

Suddenly her eyes began to beam. There was a display of red lips and white teeth, and a sort of general facial radiation. It was an effort usually fatal to guardsmen, but it affected Mr. Carteret like the turning on of an electric heater, and he backed away as if he felt the room were warm enough. "I am so glad," she said.

"Tell me," she went on in her soft, delightfully modulated voice, "aren't you interested with Mr. Barclay in some farms?"

"We own two ranches together," said Mr. Carteret.

"Yes, that was it," said Lady Withers; "and you raise horses on them?"

Mr. Carteret apprehended what was coming. "Yes; ranch horses," he said dryly.

"And such good ones, as Mr. Barclay was telling me," said Lady Withers. "He made me quite enthusiastic with his account of it all, and he is so anxious to have dear Cecil manage them in England; but before Cecil decides one way or the other I want your advice."

Mr. Carteret looked at her and stroked his mustache. His opportunity to save Barclay had come. "My advice would be worth very little," he said; "but I can give you all the facts, and of course Barclay—well, he can't."

A shade of apprehension crossed Lady Withers's face. "And why not?" she demanded.

"I should rather not go into that," said Mr. Carteret. "Of course the great objection to the scheme is that it would be unprofitable for Mr. Granvil, because no one would buy our horses."

"But wouldn't they," said Lady Withers, "if they were good ones?"

"Major Hammerslea can answer that question better than I," said Mr. Carteret. He looked toward that great man and smiled. The Major was the author of "Schooling and Riding British Hunters," and Mr. Carteret knew his views.

"No one," said the Major, impressively, "would buy an American horse if he desired to make or possess a really good hunter."

"But why advertise that they were American?" observed Lady Withers, blandly.

"How could you hide it?" said the Major.

"Exactly," said Mr. Carteret.

"Furthermore," observed the Major, his interest in the controversy growing, "the output of a single breeding institution would scarcely make it worth Cecil's while to manage an agency for their distribution."

"I think you don't understand," said Lady Withers, "that Mr. Carteret has a large place."

"My friend the Duke of Westchester," began the Major, "has in his breeding farm eight thousand acres—"

"But I've no doubt that Mr. Carteret's is very nearly as large," interrupted Lady Withers.

"I don't think size has anything to do with it," said Mr. Carteret, uneasily. "The fact is, we don't raise the kind of horse that English dealers would buy."

"I think size has much to do with it," replied the Major.

"I wish," said Lady Withers, "that you would tell Major Hammerslea exactly how large your farms are."

"I don't know exactly," said Mr. Carteret, uneasily.

"But, about how large?" insisted Lady Withers.

"There is something over a million acres in the Texas piece," said Mr. Carteret, with some embarrassment, "and something under six hundred thousand in Wyoming."

Lady Withers and the Major both looked at him with eyes of amazement. But Lady Withers's amazement was admiring.

"I thought so," said she, calmly. The Major in silence walked over to the table and took a cigar. "Looking at it from all points of view," she continued, "it would be just the thing for Cecil. He is intelligent with regard to horses."

"But I don't wish to go to Texas," said the Hon. Cecil, who had joined the group. "They say the shootin' 's most moderate."

"It isn't necessary *yet* for you to go to Texas," said Lady Withers, coldly. "Mr. Carteret and I are arranging to employ your talents in England."

"Of course another objection," said Mr. Carteret, "is that Granvil is too good a man to waste on such an occupation. The horse business is very confining. It's an awful bore to be tied down."

"You are absolutely right about that," said the Hon. Cecil, with a burst of frankness. "You don't know what a relief it is to be out of the Guards. Awfully confining life, the Guards."

"I think," said Lady Withers, apparently oblivious to the views of her nephew, "that Mr. Barclay takes rather the more businesslike view of these matters. It is he, I fancy, who looks after the affairs of your estates; and I should judge," she continued, "that, after all, his advice to a young man like Cecil with a very moderate income would be wiser. I believe very much in an occupation for young men."

Mr. Carteret saw that his time had come. He looked at Lady Withers and smiled sadly. "Of course I'm very fond of Barclay," he said in a lower tone, "and of course he is an awfully charming, plausible boy—" Then he stopped, apparently because Major Hammerslea was returning with his cigar.

"What do you mean?" asked Lady Withers.

Mr. Carteret made no direct reply, but moved toward the piano, and Lady Withers followed. "It is best to speak plainly," he said, "because, after all, business is business, as we say."

"Exactly," said Lady Withers. Her teeth had ceased to gleam. The radiance had left her face, though not the bloom upon it. Her large, beaming eyes had contracted. She looked twenty years older.

"The fact is," said Mr. Carteret, steadily, "that Barclay is not the business manager of our ranches. He is not a business man at all. It is true that he still retains a certain interest in the ranch properties but he has been so unbusinesslike that everything he's got is in the hands of a trustee. He gets his income monthly, like a remittance-man. He is not in actual want; but—"

"I see," said Lady Withers, coldly. "I had misunderstood the situation." She turned and crossed to one of the card-tables and sat down.

After she had gone, Mr. Carteret lighted a cigarette and went out. It was his intention to go to his room, have his tub, and change. His mind was relieved. He had no fear that Lady Withers would either beam or radiate for a young man whose fortune was in captivity to a trustee. He had saved Barclay, and he was pleased with himself. As he passed through the twilight of the main hallway, the front door opened, and Lady Mary Granvil and Barclay entered side by side. It was the girl's voice that he heard first.

"Please have it dressed at once," she was saying.

"But there's no hurry," said Barclay.

"Please, at once," said the girl. There was something in her tone that made Mr. Carteret turn from the stairs and go forward to meet them.

"I've snapped my collar-bone," said Barclay. "It's nothing."

The girl drew back a step into the heavy shadow of the corner, but Mr. Carteret did not notice it. "So old True Blue has put you down at last," he said.

"Yes," said Barclay evasively; "that is—"

"He was not riding True Blue," said Lady Mary resolutely. "He was riding my horse. Mr. Barclay changed with me."

"The horse was all right," said Barclay, hurriedly. "It was my own fault. I bothered him at a piece of timber. It wasn't the horse you thought it was," he added rather anxiously. "It was one they got from Oakly, the dealer."

Now, Mr. Carteret had sold the horse in question to Oakly, yet he said nothing, but stood and looked from one to the other. Disturbing suspicions were springing up in the depths of his mind.

The girl broke the silence. "You ought to get it set without any more delay," she said; "you really ought. It will begin to swell. Go up, and I shall have them telephone for the doctor."

"You are quite right," said Mr. Carteret; "but I'll see about the doctor."

He turned and started toward the end of the long hall, searching for a bell that he might summon a servant. Presently it occurred to him that he had no idea of the doctor's name, and that there might be several doctors. He stopped, turned, and came back noiselessly upon the heavy rug and all but invisible in the dusk of the unlighted hallway. Suddenly he stopped. The girl had been watching Barclay as he went up the stairs. As he passed out of sight, she turned and dropped into a chair with a little sigh, like one who has been under a strain. On the table beside her lay the silk muffler in which his arm had been tied. She took it up and began folding it. Then she smoothed it with curious little strokings and touches, and then suddenly pressing it to her cheek, put it down and disappeared through the morning-room doorway in a confusion in which she had surprised herself. Mr. Carteret stepped back behind a curtain, and when he was sure that Lady Mary was not coming back, instead of ordering the doctor, he went to Barclay's room.

"I should like to know," he began, "how it was that you were riding Mary Granvil's horse?"

Barclay met his look steadily. "I wanted to try it with a view to purchase," he answered. "You know Lady Withers had said she wished to sell it."

"Excuse me for being plain," said Mr. Carteret, "but my opinion is that no man would have ridden that horse when hounds were running unless he wanted to marry either the woman who owned it or the woman who was riding it."

"Well?" said Barclay.

"Well," said Mr. Carteret, "is it Lady Withers?"

"No," said Barclay decisively; "it isn't Lady Withers."

Mr. Carteret looked at his young friend with outward indifference. Inwardly he was experiencing much relief. "When are you going to announce your engagement?" he asked.

Barclay shook his head grimly. "I wish I knew," he said. "I'm up against it, I fancy."

"It's not my business," said Mr. Carteret, "but I should like to know what you mean."

"Why, in a word, Carty," said Barclay, "I'm not *it*, that's all, and the situation is such that I don't see what I can do to make her change her mind."

Mr. Carteret looked perplexed. What he had seen in the hall gave him a feeling of guilt. "When did she refuse you?" he asked at last.

"She hasn't refused me," answered Barclay. "You don't ask a woman to marry you when you know that she cares for some one else."

"So she cares for some one else?" observed Mr. Carteret.

"You could guess whom," said Barclay.

"Supposing she does like Brinton a bit," said Mr. Carteret, "what's to prevent you from getting into the race?"

"Can't you see!" exclaimed Barclay. "If Lady Withers thought I wanted to marry her,—you know what she'd do."

"Well," said Mr. Carteret, "if she isn't forced to marry *your* money, she'll have to marry Tappingwell-Sikes's, and, on the whole, I think she'd prefer your railroads to his beer."

"What Sikes may do," said Barclay, "is not my business; but I want no woman to marry me if she doesn't want to."

"Your sentiments are not discreditable," observed his friend; "but, after all, she may want to. You can't be sure until you ask her."

"Yes, I can," said Barclay. "Besides," he went on, "am I anything wonderful that she should jump at me?"

"That is not an original suggestion," said Mr. Carteret, thoughtfully, "yet it may be in point. However, it is a great mistake to act upon it when you are making love."

"In the second place," Barclay continued, "Captain Brinton has the inside track."

"I don't think so," said Mr. Carteret, decisively; "they're too much together in public."

Barclay shook his head dismally. "Over here it means they're engaged," he said.

"Well, what do you mean to do about it?" asked Mr. Carteret after a pause.

"What is there to do?" answered Barclay. "Nothing but wait."

"My boy," said the older man, "I'm not surprised that you're in love with Mary Granvil; I am myself, and, what's more, I'm not going to have her thrown away on a bounder like Tappingwell-Sikes. If you don't propose to her, I shall. I'll keep my hands off for three weeks, and then look out."

Barclay smiled. "You don't frighten me very much," he said.

"But I'm in earnest," said Mr. Carteret. "It's time for me to get married. I'm not the kind for a grand passion, and that's all in my favor when it comes to making love. In fact, my indifference to women is what makes me so attractive."

"Perhaps it is," said Barclay. "Generally speaking, I'm indifferent to women myself. But—"

"I'm not going to discuss it with you," said Mr. Carteret interrupting. "I'm going to propose to Mary Granvil."

He examined the broken collar-bone, sent a servant to telephone for the doctor, and left the room. "Now," he said to himself, "I've got to go to Lady Withers and *un*save Barclay." And he went back to the library where they were still having tea.

It was Lady Withers's dummy, and the cards being excessively bad, she had risen and was walking about. As Mr. Carteret entered, she glanced at him coldly; but as he continued to approach, she held her ground.

"I have just had an idea," he began with an air of mystery.

"How very interesting!" observed Lady Withers. She neither beamed nor gleamed nor radiated.

"Yes," he went on, "it suddenly dawned upon me that what you really wanted was that Cecil should have something to do."

"Really?" said Lady Withers.

"Exactly," said Carteret. He was making heavy weather, but he kept on. "You see, my first idea was that you were merely interested in bringing American horses to England, as it were, don't you see, for the humor of the thing—Haw! haw!"—he laughed painfully,—"and so, you see, I took Cecil's very natural view of the matter, that it would be a great bore, don't you see, not realizing in the least that you wished it for his own good. Now I think, if you are serious about it, which of course I never fancied, that Cecil would be just the man to manage an agency and see that the horses were broken and schooled and got ready for the dealers to buy; and more than that, I think he ought to have a large share of the profits, don't you?"

As Mr. Carteret talked on Lady Withers had obviously melted, though she had not yet begun to beam. "I must say," she said frankly, "that I do think he ought to have a large share of the profits."

"And I think," he continued, "that he ought to have a salary besides."

"It seems only reasonable," she replied, "when you think of Cecil's influence and that sort of thing, to say nothing of his experience with horses. I happen to know that Lord Glen Rossmuir got five thousand pounds merely for going upon the board of the United Marmalade and Jam Company, and he gets a salary besides."

"And Cecil is far abler than Glen Rossmuir," said Mr. Carteret.

"Far," said Lady Withers.

"And one more thing," said Mr. Carteret; "what I said about Barclay's trustee was somewhat misleading, because, don't you see, the trust comes to an end in six weeks."

"And then," said Lady Withers, "do I understand that he will have control of his own fortune?"

"Unconditionally," said Mr. Carteret. "And I may say that he is so awfully rich that to avoid beggars and anarchists he keeps his name out of the telephone-book, which in New York is something like the equivalent of being a duke in England."

"When will the first ship-load of the horses arrive?" asked Lady Withers.

Mr. Carteret was taken aback, but an idea came to him. "It has just occurred to me," he said, "that a neighbor of ours in Wyoming is sending over some horses in the course of the next few days. I could wire him and have him bring over two or three for samples—patterns, you call them; and then, if they are what you approve of, we shall have a ship-load come over."

"Excellent!" said Lady Withers. "Wire him at once, and you also had better wire your manager, so that there may be no delay."

"I will," said Mr. Carteret. "And, by the way," he added, "if Cecil should need an assistant, do you think Captain Brinton would do?"

Lady Withers thought a moment, and looked doubtful. "He's a nice boy," she said, "and without a penny; but he's so mad about Christina Dalrymple that he would be good for nothing in the way of an assistant to lighten Cecil's duties. He bores poor dear Mary nearly to death confiding his love-affairs to her."

"Then we can leave the position of assistant manager open," said Mr. Carteret.

"It would be better," said Lady Withers. She began to beam again. "In fact, I have another nephew; but I must play," she added, and went back to the card-table. "Cecil," she observed, before the hand began, "there will be some of Mr. Barclay's horses delivered at the Hall in a fortnight from now. Will you make your plans to be there for a few days?"

The Hon. Cecil was dealing, but he stopped. "I tell you it's all rubbish, these American horses," he said petulantly. "And besides, they buck like devils. It's an awful bore."

"Not any more than any young thoroughbred horses might buck," said Mr. Carteret. "They may kick and play, but it's nothing."

"Cecil is only joking about the bucking," said a soft voice from the chimney-corner. It was Lady Mary. "Cecil can ride anything that was ever saddled," she added.

"Still, it is a bore," said the Hon. Cecil, only partly mollified by the sisterly compliment.

"One word," said Mr. Carteret in an undertone to Cecil. "Please tell Lady Withers that I'm going to buy that horse your sister was riding."

"Good horse," said the Hon. Cecil, and he went on with his dealing.

Mr. Carteret did not add that he was going to have him shot and fed to the hounds. Instead, he went back to the fireplace, where the gray eyes were gleaming in the firelight.

"You mustn't keep Mr. Carteret from cabling," Lady Withers called from the bridge-table; "and while I think of it," she added, "won't you and Mr. Barclay come to Crumpeton for a week as soon as the horses arrive? I shall write you. Do you think that Mr. Barclay will be able to come?"

"I think it probable," said Mr. Carteret.

The firelight suddenly ceased to gleam upon the gray eyes. They were turned toward the floor.

"That is very nice," said Lady Withers, arranging her cards; "but you mustn't let me detain you. You know they might just miss a steamer."

"I'm off," said Mr. Carteret, and he left the room.

The party at Mrs. Ascott-Smith's dispersed next day. Mr. Carteret went back to his own house, which he had done over in the American manner, to get warm, and to have a bath in a porcelain tub. Barclay returned with him to nurse his collar-bone. As he was unable to hunt, he went to the meets in a motor, and watched for the slim little figure in the weather-beaten habit. What he saw neither cheered nor reassured him.

"It is very natural," he said gloomily to Mr. Carteret, "but there are at least a dozen men after her. Besides Sikes, there were four guardsmen who rode to cover with her, and then old Lord Watermere butted in. He's looking for a third wife. You know yourself that when a man pays any attention to a woman out hunting it's because he likes her."

"I don't know what their intentions are," said Mr. Carteret; "but as far as I am concerned, you have three weeks less one day in which to propose to her. I want to do the fair thing," he continued, "and I advise you that the psychological moment would be while the collar-bone is a novelty. There is an American buggy in the stable, and an American trotting horse that drives with one hand. *Verb sap.*"

"But it isn't done in England," said Barclay.

"Buggy-riding," said Mr. Carteret, "or its equivalent, is done wherever there is a man of spirit and a young lady with intuitions. The trouble with you," he went on, "is that you are too modest on the one hand and too self-important on the other. If you are not good enough for the girl, you needn't fear that Lady Withers will give you the preference over Sikes. This is the last advice I'm going to give. Henceforth I act on my own account."

Barclay smiled doubtfully, but said nothing.

"I mean it," said Mr. Carteret.

That afternoon at tea a telegram arrived from which Barclay gathered that his mother was in Paris, afflicted with a maid with chicken-pox, and that she was frantic with the sanitary regulations of the French government.

"Couldn't I go?" said Mr. Carteret.

"No," said Barclay, "there are twenty-eight words in this dispatch. It is a hurry-call for me." He took the night train.

Three weeks later he came back. He arrived late in the afternoon and found his host before the fire looking thoughtfully at a note which he held in his hand. "I'm glad to see you back," said Mr. Carteret. "Have you proposed to Mary Granvil?"

"I?" said Barclay. "No. How could I in Paris? Why?" There was an anxiety in his manner which suggested that he was not as resigned as he said he was.

"If you haven't been bungling," said Mr. Carteret, "blessed if I know what has happened."

"Is it announced?" asked Barclay. "Is it Sikes?"

"Read Lady Withers's note," said Mr. Carteret.

Barclay took the note and read:

> DEAR MR. CARTERET:
>
> You will doubtless not be surprised at my request that you remove your horses at once from my stables. It is a disappointment to me that an unforeseen change in my plans makes it impossible for me to have you and Mr. Barclay at Crumpeton this week.
>
> Sincerely yours,
> CONSTANTIA GRANVIL WITHERS.

"It's Sikes," said Barclay.

"It may be," said Mr. Carteret. "I ought to have taken the matter into my own hands a week ago."

"You don't mean you are in earnest?" said Barclay.

"You will very soon find out," said Mr. Carteret. "I have no false delicacy about proposing to a lady merely because I'm not sure she's in love with me."

At ten o'clock the next morning he and Barclay were sitting in the motor in front of Crumpeton, while a footman explained that the ladies were at the stables and Major Hammerslea was with them. Mr. Carteret told the chauffeur to go to the stables, and there they got out. Standing saddled on the floor of an open box-stall was a showy-looking chestnut thoroughbred horse. As was only natural, the occupants of the motor stopped to examine him, and Mr. Carteret gave an exclamation of surprise. "If I am not mistaken," he said, "that is one of our Prince Royal colts." He looked carefully at the inside of the foreleg just below the armpit, and found a small brand. "It is," he announced. "By Jove! he *is* a good-looker!"

While he was doing this, Lady Withers's stud groom, Tripp, came out and touched his cap. "'E's a nice one, sir," said Tripp.

"He is," said Mr. Carteret. "Is the other one as good?"

"Other one, sir?" said Tripp. "Wot other?"

"The other American horse that came with him," said Mr. Carteret.

"This one only come 'alf an hour ago," said Tripp. "'E's Major Hammerslea's 'oss. 'E bought 'im last week at Tattersalls."

"You must be mistaken, Tripp," said Barclay; "this is one of the horses that we had sent out to Mr. Cecil."

"Beggin' your pardon, sir," said Tripp; "this is *not* one of the 'osses sent out to Mr. Cecil; this is Major Hammerslea's 'oss. The hanimals that arrived from America are in the lower stables."

"Thank you," said Mr. Carteret; and they passed on in the direction indicated by Tripp. "There is no use wasting breath on that blockhead," he said to Barclay.

In the court of the lower stables they came upon Lady Withers and the Major inspecting some two-year-olds.

"Good morning," said Mr. Carteret. "I gathered from your note that you are dissatisfied with the horses. Would it be too much to tell me why?"

"It was my idea," said Lady Withers coldly, "that Cecil should undertake the management of a horse agency, not a zoo."

"I am still in the dark," said Mr. Carteret, "but you speak as if they had given you some trouble."

"My dear fellow," said the Major, "it has turned out precisely as I said it would."

"But it can't be anything very serious," said Mr. Carteret.

"Oh, no—it is nothing serious," said Lady Withers, "to have two grooms in the hospital with fractured limbs, and to have no insurance upon them, to have Cecil bitten in the shoulder, to have my breaking harness torn to pieces and Tripp giving me notice. No one would consider that serious."

"There must be some mistake about this," said Mr. Carteret blankly. "As I told you, these horses were apt to buck playfully, but, if properly handled, would cause no trouble."

"It may be playfulness," said Lady Withers; "I saw one of them buck the saddle over his forelegs and head."

"That is a fact," said the Major. "I had read of such a thing, but had never believed it possible."

"It is possible," said Mr. Carteret, "but not with our horses."

"My dear sir," said the Major, "as I was saying to Lady Withers, your horses may be very good horses in their own place in America, but they are not at all according to English ideas."

"At the same time," observed Mr. Carteret with some heat, "I noticed that you are riding one of them."

The Major looked at him in amazement. "I ride an American horse! What do you mean, sir?" he demanded.

"The chestnut horse," began Mr. Carteret, with a gesture toward the upper stable.

"The chestnut horse," said the Major, "I bought at Tattersalls three days ago. I know nothing about him except that he was quite the image of Prince Royal, a great sire that I once owned."

"That is hardly surprising," said Mr. Carteret; "Prince Royal is his father. I'm certain about it because he's marked with our Prince Royal brand."

The Major and Lady Withers looked at Mr. Carteret, and then at each other. Their eyes seemed to say, "We must humor this person until attendants from the madhouse can be brought to secure him."

"Perhaps," said Lady Withers, "you would care to see *your* horses."

"I should like to see the other one," he answered stubbornly, and they went into the stable.

Lady Withers paused before a box-stall which was boarded up to the ceiling. She cautiously opened the upper half of the door, and peered through the grating. Inside was a strange, thick-shouldered, goose-rumped, lop-eared brown creature covered with shaggy wool. It stood on three legs, and carried its head low like a member of the cat family.

"To me," said Lady Withers, "it looks like a bear; but I am assured that it is a horse. I would advise you not to go near it. This is the one that bit dear Cecil."

The two Americans gazed in amazement.

"A charming type of hunter!" observed Lady Withers.

Mr. Carteret made no reply. He was trying to think it out, but was making no headway. While thus engaged his eyes wandered down the stable passage, and he saw one of his own grooms approaching. Almost anything was pleasanter than contemplating the creature in the box-stall, so he watched the man approach. "I beg pardon, sir," said the man, "but the butler sent me to find you, sir, with a telegram that came just after you had left."

Mr. Carteret tore open the envelop and read the message, which was a long one. As he finished a slight sigh escaped him. "This may interest the Major," he observed, "and possibly explain various things." He handed the despatch to Lady Withers, who opened her lorgnette and began to read it to the Major.

> Police have Jim Siddons, one of our horse foremen. Has been drunk for week. Confesses he sold your horses at auction, but don't know where. Believes he shipped you two outlaws. "Smallpox," brand, "arrow V," and "Hospital," brand, "bar O." Hospital dangerous horse. Killed three men. Look out. Very sorry.
>
> REILLY.

"Who is Reilly?" asked Lady Withers.

"Reilly," said Mr. Carteret, "is the horse superintendent of Buffalo Bill's show. You see Buffalo Bill is the neighbor to whom I cabled."

"Then—" began Lady Withers, but the Major interrupted her.

"Does this mean," he demanded, "that I have bought a stolen horse?"

"It means," said Mr. Carteret, "that if you will accept an American horse from Mr. Barclay and myself, we shall be very much flattered."

"Really,—" said the Major. He began to enter upon one of his discourses, but stopped as he saw that neither Mr. Carteret nor Barclay was listening. Instead, they were trying to make out the brand on the creature in the box-stall.

"I can see the end of the arrow," said Mr. Carteret. "This is Smallpox. Where is the bad one—Hospital?"

"Where is the other one?" asked Lady Withers of a stable-boy.

"In the back stable yard, your Ladyship," said the boy. "Lady Mary is riding him."

Each one of the four looked at the other speechless with horror.

"Lady Mary!" gasped the Major.

Mr. Carteret and Barclay started for the back stable yard, but Barclay got there first. As he was opening the gate, Mr. Carteret caught up. "Keep your head," he observed. There were sounds of hoof-beats, exclamations from grooms and other indications of battle. They went in and saw Lady Mary sitting on the back of a creature rather more hairy and unpleasant-looking than Smallpox. Her face was pink with exertion, but otherwise she looked as neat, unruffled, and slim as she always did in the saddle. Hospital had paused, panting, and was trying to look at her out of the back of his eyes in sour wonder. He was not defeated. He was merely surprised that his preliminary exhibition had not left him alone with the saddle. When there was only the saddle to get rid of he usually got down to business and "bucked some," as they say in Western regions.

Lady Mary nodded as they entered, and her lips parted in a little smile.

"Good morning," said Mr. Carteret. He saw that the situation was serious and fraught with difficulties. And there was no time to be lost. "I've something extremely important to tell you," he said in a matter-of-fact tone. "Will you be good enough to get your leg well clear of the pommel and slip off that horse?"

"Well, really," said the girl, laughing, "it is so unpleasant getting on that I should rather you told me as I am."

"I will explain afterward," said Mr. Carteret, "but you would oblige me very much by slipping off that horse immediately."

The girl looked at him. "I see through you," she said, "you are afraid I'll get bucked off."

"It would be no disgrace," he answered; "you are not sitting on a horse, but on an explosion."

"It would be a disgrace to get off because you were afraid," said the girl. "Besides," she continued in a lower voice, "I'm very sorry for the way in which my aunt and Cecil have acted in this matter. You warned them that the horses might buck playfully. You know the Granvils are supposed to ride." She broke off and spoke to the horse, for Hospital had satisfied his curiosity as to the newcomers, and was walking sidewise, deciding whether he would buck some more or roll over.

Barclay started for the brute's head, but his good arm was seized and he was thrust back. "My dear girl," said Mr. Carteret, going a step closer, "if you have any feelings of humanity,"—he looked very grave, but there was a smile in his eyes, and he spoke in a low voice, which nevertheless was plainly audible to Barclay,—"I say, if you have any feelings of humanity," he repeated, "or any sense of the fitness of things, get off that horse at once. Here is a young man with a bad arm and something extremely important on his mind that is for your ear alone, and he'll unquestionably get killed if he goes near enough that horse to tell you about it. Be a good girl," he added in a whisper, "and be kind to him. Perhaps he's worth it." A quick flush came into the girl's face. And Mr. Carteret, without glancing back, hurried out of the paddock.

Just outside the gate he ran into Lady Withers, the Major, and Mr. Tappingwell-Sikes, who had just arrived. They had been following as fast as they could.

"What has happened?" demanded the Major, much out of breath.

"I don't know," said Mr. Carteret; "but we'll all know in a few minutes."

Lady Withers looked at him in amazement, and tried to brush past; but he barred the way. "There is nothing you can do," he said. "If she chooses to stay on Hospital, it's too late to get her off without a breeches-buoy. If she got down, these are moments when she mustn't be interrupted."

"Are you mad?" said Lady Withers, "or am I?"

"Neither of us is mad," said Mr. Carteret, "but I have just proposed to Lady Mary, and I am anxious to see what she is going to do about it."

Lady Withers's mouth half opened in astonishment.

"You have proposed!" she exclaimed, but that was all. She looked at Mr. Tappingwell-Sikes, and then again at Mr. Carteret.

"Perhaps," said the Major, "it would be well for Mr. Sikes and me to withdraw."

"Your presence is very agreeable at all times," said Mr. Carteret; "but really there is nothing that you can do." The Major and Mr. Tappingwell-Sikes withdrew.

"But I didn't know that you were interested in Mary," said Lady Withers, coming to her senses. "Perhaps I had better have a word with her. The dear child is so young that she may not know her own mind."

"I think she does by this time," he replied. The gate opened, and Barclay and Mary Granvil stood in the gateway. "I'm rather sure of it," he added. "You can see for yourself."

"But—" said Lady Withers, looking accusingly at Mr. Carteret. She was fairly dumfounded.

"It was I that proposed," said Mr. Carteret, "but the beneficiary is apparently Barclay."

"It is," said Barclay.

All Lady Withers could do was to gasp hysterically, "How very American!"

"Not at all," said Mr. Carteret. "The vicarious proposal is essentially European. I think," he added, "all that remains for you to do is to confer your blessing."

As Lady Withers gazed at her niece she saw in those gray Granvil eyes the magical light that is so sad to those that are without it, and she saw in her face the loveliness and other consequences of being sweet. The ghosts of what she herself might have had and what she herself might have been thronged back to her. Her hard, world-scarred heart trembled; tears stood in her eyes, and without speaking and without a single false beam or sparkle she took the girl to her breast and kissed her.

Mr. Carteret turned away and followed the Major and Tappingwell-Sikes. There was something in his throat that he felt would make it difficult for him to contribute anything illuminating to the situation.

III
MR. CARTERET'S ADVENTURE WITH A LOCKET

Mrs. Ascott-Smith knew that Mr. Carteret had been attentive to Miss Rivers, but she had never known how attentive. She never suspected that the affair had reached the point of an engagement, subsequently broken by Miss Rivers. If she had known the facts, she would not have invited Mr. Carteret to Chilliecote Abbey when Miss Rivers and Captain Wynford were there.

Yet the presence of Miss Rivers and Wynford was not the reason that Mr. Carteret gave himself for declining the invitation. He did not dread meeting Miss Rivers; she was nothing to him but a mistake and an old friend. Whether she married Wynford or some other man, it was the same to him. The affair was over. He even had it in mind to get married before very long, if only to prove it.

He was in such a mood as he walked down the passage to the smoking-room with Mrs. Ascott-Smith's note crumpled in his hand. His eyes looked straight before him and saw nothing. Behind him there followed the soft, whispering tread of cushioned feet, and that he did not hear. Perhaps it was not because he was absorbed that he did not hear it, for it was always following him, and he had ceased to note it, as one ceases to note the clock ticking. But as he sat down, he felt the touch of a cold nose on his hand and one little lick. He glanced down, and looked into the sad, wistful eyes of the wire-haired fox terrier. With this, Penwiper dropped gravely upon the floor, gazing up adoring and mournful, yet content. Mr. Carteret was used to this idolatry, as he was used to the patter of the following footsteps, but on this occasion it provoked speculation. It occurred to him to wonder how in a just universe a devotion like Penwiper's would be repaid. Then he wondered if, after all, it was a just universe. If so, why should Penwiper have that look chronically in his eyes?

Presently Mr. Carteret got up and took the newspapers. He was annoyed with himself and annoyed with Penwiper. It was the dog that called up these disquieting ideas. The dog was irrevocably associated with Miss Rivers. He had given her Penwiper as an engagement present, and when the affair ended, she had sent him back. He ought not to have taken him back. He felt that it had been a great mistake to become interested again in Penwiper, as it had been a great mistake to become interested at all in Miss Rivers. He continued to peruse the newspapers till he found that he was reading a paragraph for the third time. Then he got up and went out to the stables.

March was drawing to a close, and with it the hunting season, when there dawned one of those celestial mornings that are appropriate to May, but in England sometimes appear earlier. It brought to the meet five hundred

English ladies and gentlemen, complaining that it was too hot to hunt. In this great assemblage Mr. Carteret found himself riding about, saying "good morning," automatically inquiring of Lady Martingale about the chestnut mare's leg, parrying Mrs. Cutcliffe's willingness to let him a house, and avoiding Captain Coper's anxiety to sell him a horse. He was not aware that he was restless or that he threaded his way through one group after another, acting as usually he did not act, until Major Hammerslea asked him if he was looking for his second horseman. Then he rode off by himself, and stood still. He had seen pretty much everybody that was out, yet he had come upon none of the Chilliecote party. However, as he asked himself twice, "What was that to him?"

A few minutes later they jogged on to covert and began to draw. A fox went away, the hounds followed him for two fields, then flashed over and checked. After that they could make nothing of it. The fox-hunting authorities said that there was no scent.

At two o'clock they were pottering about Tunbarton Wood, having had a disappointing morning. The second horsemen came up with sandwich-boxes, and, scattered in groups among the broad rides, people ate lunch, smoked, enjoyed the sunshine, and grumbled at the weather, which made sport impossible. And then the unexpected happened, as in fox-hunting it usually does. Hounds found in a far corner of the wood, and disappeared on a burning scent before any one could get to them. Instantly the world seemed to be filled with people galloping in all directions, inquiring where hounds had gone, and receiving no satisfactory answer. Experience had taught Mr. Carteret that under such conditions the most unfortunate thing to do is to follow others who know as little as one's self. Accordingly he opened a hand gate, withdrew a few yards into a secluded lane, pulled up, and tried to think like a fox. This idea had been suggested by Mr. Kipling's Gloucester fisherman who could think like a cod. While he was thinking, he saw a great many people gallop by in the highway in both directions. He noted Major Hammerslea, who was apt to be conspicuous when there was hard riding on the road, leading a detachment of people north. He noted Lady Martingale, who liked fences better than roads, leading a charge south. And following Lady Martingale he noted Captain Wynford. Apparently, then, the Abbey people were out, after all. "Perhaps Mrs. Ascott-Smith will turn up," he said to himself, and he followed Wynford with his eyes until he was out of sight, but saw neither Mrs. Ascott-Smith nor any one else who might have been under his escort.

After a while there were no more people going by in either direction. Something like a sigh escaped him; then he lit a cigarette.

"If I were the hunted fox," he said to himself, "I think I should have circled over Crumpelow Hill, and then bent south with the idea of getting to ground in Normanhurst Wood. I'll take a try at it."

He rode off down the lane to the eastward, riding slowly, for there was no hurry. If he was right, he would be ahead of the fox. If he was wrong, he was so far behind that it made no difference what he did. So he jogged on up and down hill, and smoked. He rode thus for about two miles when his hope began to wither. On every side stretched the winter-green, rolling country fenced into a patchwork of great pastures. In the distance, to the south, lay the brown-gray mass of Normanhurst Wood. The landscape was innocent of any gleam of scarlet coat or black figure of horseman on hilltop against the sky.

"I'm wrong," he said half aloud. "I guess I could think better as a codfish than as a fox."

A moment later he saw fresh hoof-prints crossing the lane in front of him, and it burst upon him that his theory was right, but that he was too late. A dozen people must have crossed. They had come into the lane through a hand gate, and had jumped out over some rails that mended a gap in the tall, bushy hedge. Beside the hoof-prints was the evidence of a rail that was freshly broken. He contemplated the situation judicially.

"How far behind I am," he said to himself, "I do not know; whether these people are following hounds or Lady Martingale I do not know: but anything is better than going down this interminable lane." So he put his horse at the place where the rail was broken. The next instant, the horse, which was overfed and under-exercised, jumped high over the low rail, and jammed his hat against an overhanging bough, and, on landing, ran away. When Mr. Carteret got him in hand, they were well out into the field, and he began to look along the farther fence for a place to jump out.

In doing this he noticed at the end of the long pasture a horse grazing, and it looked to him as if the horse were saddled. He glanced around, expecting to see an unhappy man stalking a lost mount, but there was no one in sight. So he rode toward the horse. As he came nearer he saw that the saddle was a woman's. The horse made no attempt to run away, and Mr. Carteret caught it. One glance showed him that there was mud on its ears, mud on its rump, and that one of the pommels was broken. Immediately, although he had never seen horse or saddle before, a strange and unreasonable apprehension seized him. He felt that it was Miss Rivers's horse; and yet his common sense told him that the idea was absurd. She was probably not out hunting, and if she were, the chances were a thousand to one against it being she. Nevertheless, he opened the sandwich-box strapped to the saddle and took out the silver case. It bore the inscription S. R. from C. C. If he could believe his eyes, the thousand-to-one chance had come off.

He looked about him dazed. There was no one in sight.

"It must have happened back a way," he said half aloud, "and the horse followed the hunt."

Mounting, he led it by its bridle-reins, and began to gallop toward the place where the fence had been broken. Approaching the broken rail, he began to pull up when his eye caught something dark upon the grass close to the hedge.

One look, and he saw that it was a woman and that it was Sally Rivers. She was lying on her back, motionless, her white face looking up, her arms at her side, almost as if she were asleep. The apprehensive intuition that had come to him at the sight of the broken saddle came again and told him that she was dead. It must be so. That afternoon they were in the grasp of one of those terrible pranks of fate that are told as strange "true stories."

But she was not dead. He realized it when he bent over her and took her pulse. It was reasonably strong. The injury was obviously a concussion, for her hat lay beside her, crushed and torn off by the fall. Her breathing, though hardly normal, was not alarming, and it seemed to be growing deeper and more peaceful even as he watched. There were indications that she would come to presently. After all, it was only such an accident as claims its daily victim in the hunting countries. It was nothing to be alarmed about. As the strain relaxed, he became aware of its tensity. He was limp now, and shaking like a leaf, and then the question put itself to him, Was this because he had found a woman that he believed dead or because that woman was Sally Rivers? There was only one honest answer. He made it, and in his inner heart he was glad.

She was not dead. He realized it when he bent over her

Nevertheless, he still protested that it was absurd, that the affair was over. Even if there were no Wynford, he knew that she would never change her mind; and, then, there was Wynford. Even now he was sitting beside her only because her eyes were sightless, because she herself was away. When she came back, it would be trespass to remain. He was in another's place. It was Wynford who ought to have found her.

If he could have stolen away he would have done so. But that being impossible, he fell to watching her as if she were not herself, but a room that she had once lived in—a room that he too had known, that was delightful with associations and fragrant with faint memory-stirring perfumes. And yet, though the tenant seemed to be away, was it not after all her very self that was before him? There was the treasure of her brown hair, with the gold light in it, tumbled in heaps about her head; there was the face that had been for him the loveliness of early morning in gardens, that had haunted him in the summer perfume of clover-fields and in the fragrance of night-wrapped lawns. There was the slim, rounded figure that once had brought the blood into his face as it brushed against him. There were the hands whose touch was so smooth and cool and strong. Presently he found himself wiping the mud from her cheek as if he were enacting a ritual over some holy thing. He looked around. No human being was in sight. The afternoon sun shone mildly. In the hedgerow some little birds twittered pleasantly, and sang their private little songs.

Suddenly she opened her eyes. She looked up at him, knew him, and smiled.

"Hello, Carty," she said in her low, vibrant tones. A thrill ran through him. It was the way it used to be.

"You've had a bad fall," he said. "How do you feel?"

A little laugh came into her eyes. "How do I look?" she murmured.

"You're coming out all right," he said; "but you mustn't talk just yet."

"If I want to," she said slowly. Her eyes laughed again. "If I want to, I'll talk."

"No," said Mr. Carteret.

"Hear him boss!" she murmured. She looked up at him for a moment, and then her eyes closed. But it was not the same. The lashes lay more lightly, and a tinge of color had come into her cheeks. He sat and watched her, his mind a confusion, a great gladness in his heart.

In a little while she opened her eyes as before. "Hello, Carty," she began, but Mr. Carteret's attention was attracted by the sound of wheels in the lane. He saw an old pha\EBton, driven by a farmer, coming toward them.

The man saw him, and stopped. "Is this the place where a lady was hurt?" he asked.

"Yes," said Mr. Carteret. "How did you know?"

"A boy told me," said the farmer.

"I see," said Mr. Carteret.

At first she was independent and persisted in walking to the trap by herself. But as they drove off, she began to sway, and caught herself on his arm. After a moment she looked at him helplessly; a little smile shone in her eyes and curved the corners of her mouth. At the next jolt her head settled peacefully upon his shoulder. Her eyes closed. She seemed to be asleep.

They drove on at a walk, the led horses following. The shadows lengthened, the gold light of the afternoon grew more golden. They passed through the ancient village of Tibberton and heard the rooks calling in the parsonage trees. They passed through Normanhurst Park, under oaks that may have sheltered Robin Hood, and the rooks were calling there. In the silent stretches of the road they heard the first thrushes and the evening singing of the warblers. And every living thing, bird, tree, and grass, bore witness that it was spring.

For two hours Mr. Carteret hardly breathed. He was riding in the silver bubble of a dream; a breath, and it might be gone. At the Abbey, perforce, there was an end of it. He roused her quietly, and she responded. She was able to walk up the steps on his arm, and stood till the bell was answered. When he left her in the confusion inside she gave him her hand. It had the same cool, smooth touch as of old, but its strength was gone. It lay in his hand passive till he released it. "Good night," he said, and hurrying out, he mounted his horse and rode away. He passed some people coming back from hunting, and they seemed vague and unreal. He seemed unreal himself. He almost doubted if the whole thing were not illusion; but on the shoulder of his scarlet coat clung a thread that glistened as the evening sun fell upon it, and a fragrance that went into his blood like some celestial essence.

When he got home, the afterglow was dying in the west. The rooks were hushed, the night was already falling, and the lamps were lit. As he passed through his hallway, there came the touch of a cold nose and the one little lick upon his hand. "Get down, Penwiper," he said unthinkingly, and went on.

That week, before they let her see people, Mr. Carteret lived in a world that had only its outward circumstances in the world where others lived. He made no attempt to explain it or to justify it or yet to leave it. Several of his friends noticed the change in him, and ascribed it to the vague abstraction of biliousness.

It was a raw Sunday afternoon and he was standing before the fire in the Abbey library, when Miss Rivers came noiselessly, unexpectedly, in. Mrs. Ascott-Smith, who was playing piquet with the Major, started up in surprise. Miss Rivers had been ordered not to leave her room till the next day.

"But I'm perfectly well," said the girl; "I couldn't stand it any longer. They wouldn't so much as tell me the day of the month." Then for the first time she saw Mr. Carteret. "Why, Carty!" she exclaimed. "How nice it is to see you!"

"Thank you," he answered. Their eyes met, and he felt his heart beating. As for Miss Rivers, she flushed, dropped her eyes, and turned to Mrs. Ascott-Smith.

"My dear young lady," said the Major, impressively, as he glanced through his cards, "it is highly imprudent of you to disobey the doctor. Always obey the doctor. I once knew a charming young lady—"

"I hope I'm not rude," she interrupted, "but I might as well die of concussion as die of being bored."

"But you had such a very bad toss, my dear," said Mrs. Ascott-Smith.

"What one doesn't remember, doesn't trouble one," observed the girl. "In a sense it hasn't happened." She paused and then went on with a carelessness that was a little overdone: "What did happen, anyway? The usual things, I fancy? I suppose somebody picked me up and brought me home."

Mr. Carteret's face was a mask.

"But you remember that!" exclaimed Mrs. Ascott-Smith.

"I don't remember anything," said Miss Rivers, "until one evening I woke up in bed and heard the rooks calling in the park."

"My dear," said Mrs. Ascott-Smith, "you said good-by to him in the hallway, and thanked him, and then you walked up-stairs with a footman at your elbow."

"That is very strange," said Miss Rivers. "I *don't* remember. Who was it that I said good-by to? Whom did I thank?"

Mr. Carteret walked toward the window as if he were watching the pheasant that was strutting across the lawn.

Mrs. Ascott-Smith folded her cards in her hand and looked at the girl in amazement. "Mr. Carteret found you in a field," she said, "not far from Crumpelow Hill and brought you home. You said good-by to him."

At the mention of Mr. Carteret's name the girl's hand felt for the back of a chair, as if to steady herself. Then, as the color rushed into her face, aware of it, she stepped back into the shadow. Mrs. Ascott-Smith continued to gaze. Presently Miss Rivers turned to Mr. Carteret. "This is a surprise to me," she said in a voice like ice. "How much I am in your debt, you better than any one can understand."

He turned as if a blow had struck him, and looked at her. Her eyes met his unflinchingly, colder than her words, withering with resentment and contempt. Mrs. Ascott-Smith opened her cards again and began to count: "Tierce to the king and a point of five," she muttered vaguely. Her mind and the side glance of her eyes were upon the girl and the young man. What did it mean? "A point of five," she repeated.

Mr. Carteret hesitated a moment; he feared to trust his voice. Then he gathered himself and bowed to Mrs. Ascott-Smith. "I have people coming to tea; I must be off. Good night." His impulse was to pass the girl with the formality of a bow, but he checked it. With an effort he stopped. "Good night," he said and put out his hand. Her eyes met his without a glimmer of expression. She was looking through him into nothing. His hand dropped to his side. His face grew white. He went on and out. As the door closed behind him he heard Mrs. Ascott-Smith counting for the third time, "Tierce to the king, and a point of five."

He reached his house. In his own hallway he was giving orders that he was not at home when he felt the cold nose and the one little lick, and looking down, he saw the sad eyes fixed upon his. He went down the passageway to the smoking-room, and the patter of following feet was at his heels. He closed the door, dropped into a chair, gave a nod of assent, and Penwiper jumped into his arms.

When he could think, he constructed many explanations for the mystery of her behavior, and dismissed them successively because they did not explain. Why she should resent so bitterly his having brought her home was inexplicable on any other ground than that she was still out of her head. He would insist upon an explanation, but, after all, what difference could it make? Whatever reason there might be, the important fact was that she had acted as she had. That was the only fact which mattered. Her greeting of him when she first opened her eyes, the drive home, the parting in the hallway, were all things that had never happened for her. For him they were only dreams. He must force them out into the dim region of forgotten things.

On the next Tuesday he saw her at the meet—came upon her squarely, so that there was no escaping. She was pale and sick-looking, and was driving herself in a pony trap. He lifted his hat, but she turned away. After he had ridden by, he turned back and, stopping just behind her, slipped off his horse. "Sally," he said, "I want to speak to you."

She looked around with a start. "I should prefer not," she answered.

"You must," he said. "I have a right—"

"Do you talk to me about your right?" she said. Her gray eyes flashed.

He met her anger steadily. "I do," he replied. "You can't treat me in this way."

"How else do you deserve to be treated?" she demanded fiercely.

"What do you mean?" he said.

"You know what I mean," she retorted. "You know what you did."

"What I did!" he exclaimed. "What have I done?"

"Why do you act this way, Carty?" she said wearily. "Why do you make matters worse?"

He looked at her in perplexity. "Don't you believe me," he said, "when I tell you that I don't know what you mean?"

"How can I believe you," she answered, "when I have the proof that you do?"

"The proof?" he echoed. "What proof?"

His blank surprise shook her confidence for an instant. "You know well enough," she said. "You forgot to put back the violet."

"The violet?" he repeated. "In Heaven's name what are you talking about?"

She studied his face. Again her conviction was shaken, and she trembled in spite of herself. But she saw no other way. "I can't believe you," she said sadly.

He made no answer, but a change came over his face. His patience had gone. His anger was kindling. It began to frighten her. She summoned her will and made an effort to hold her ground. "Will you swear," she said—"will you swear you didn't open the locket?"

Still he made no reply.

"Nor shut it?" she went on. She was pleading now.

"Sally," he said in a strange voice, "I neither opened nor closed nor saw a locket. What has a locket to do with this?"

She looked at him blankly in terror, for suddenly she knew that he was speaking the truth. "Then what has happened?" she murmured.

"You must tell that," he said.

"I only know this," she began: "I wore a locket the day of the accident. There was a pressed flower in it." The color began to rise in her cheeks again. "When I came to, the flower was gone, so I knew the locket had been opened."

For a moment he was speechless. "And you treat me as you have," he cried, "on the suspicion of my opening this locket!"

She made no answer.

He laughed harshly. "You think of me as a man who would open your locket!"

Still she made no answer.

His voice dropped to a whisper. "O Sally! Sally!" he exclaimed.

"There are things on my side!" she said protestingly at last. "You can't understand because you don't know what was in the locket."

"I could guess," he said.

She went on, ignoring his remark: "And you have no explanation as to how it was opened and closed again. What am I to think?"

"Sally," he said more gently, "isn't it possible that the locket was shaken open when you fell and that the people who put you to bed closed it?"

"My maid put me to bed," said the girl; "she says the locket when she saw it was closed."

"Then perhaps the flower was lost before, and you had forgotten," he suggested.

She shook her head. "No," she answered, "the maid found the flower when she undressed me. She gave it to me when I came to. That is how my attention was called to it."

"Then strange as it seems," he said calmly, "the thing must have jarred open, the flower dropped out, and the locket shut again of itself. There is no other way."

"Perhaps," she said.

"Perhaps!" he repeated. "What other way could there have been?"

"There couldn't have been any other way," she assented, "if you say you didn't see it when you loosened my habit."

He looked at her in amazement. "Loosened your habit?" he asked.

"Yes," she said; "you loosened my habit when I was hurt."

"No," he answered.

"Do you mean to say," she demanded, "that you didn't loosen and cut things?"

"Most certainly not," he replied.

"But, Carty," she exclaimed, "some one did! Who was it?"

Just then Lady Martingale rode up to inquire how Miss Rivers was recovering, and Mr. Carteret mounted and rode away. The hounds were starting off to draw Brinkwater gorse, but he rode in the opposite direction toward Crumpelow Hill. There he found the farmer who had brought them home. Through him he found the boy who had summoned the farmer, and from the boy, as he had hoped, he discovered a clew. And then he fell to wondering why he was so bent upon clearing the matter up. At most it could only put him where he was before the day of the accident. It could not make that drive home real or make what she had said that afternoon her utterance. She would acquit him of prying into her affairs, but beyond that there was nothing to hope. Everything that he had recently learned strengthened his conviction that she was going to marry Wynford. It was a certainty. Nevertheless, from Crumpelow Hill he rode toward the Abbey.

It was nearly four o'clock when Miss Rivers came in. He rose and bowed with a playful, exaggerated ceremony. "I have come," he began, in a studiedly light key, "because I have solved the mystery."

"I am glad you have come," she said.

"It is simple," he went on. "Another man picked you up, and put you where I found you. Your breathing must have been bad, and he loosened your clothes. Probably the locket had flown open and he shut it. Then he went after a trap. Why he did not come back, I don't know."

"But I do," said Miss Rivers.

He looked at her warily, suspecting a trap for the man's name. He preferred not to mention that.

"I know," she went on, "because he has told me. He did come back part way—till he saw that you were with me."

Mr. Carteret looked at her in surprise.

"More than that," she went on, "the locket had jarred open and he saw what was in it and closed it. Perhaps that was why he went away. Anyway, after thinking about it, he decided that it was best to tell me. If he had only done so before!"

"I see," said Mr. Carteret. He did not see at all, but it was a matter about which he felt that he could not ask questions.

"You know," she said, after a pause, "that the man was Captain Wynford."

"Yes," he answered shortly. His tone changed. "Wynford is a good man—a good man," he said awkwardly. "I can congratulate you both honestly." He

paused. "Well, I must go," he went on. "I'm glad things are right again all round. Good-by." He crossed to the door, and she stood watching him. She had grown very pale.

"Carty," she said suddenly, in a dry voice, "I'm not acting well."

He looked back perplexed, but in a moment he understood. She evidently felt that she ought to tell him outright that she was going to marry Wynford.

"In treating you as I did," she finished, "in judging you—"

"You were hasty," he said, "but I can understand."

She shook her head. "You can't understand if you think that there was only a flower in the locket."

"Perhaps I have guessed already that there was a picture," he said—"a picture that was not for my eyes."

She looked at him gravely. "No," she said, "you haven't guessed. I don't think you've guessed; and when I think how I misjudged you, how harsh I was, I want you to see it. It is almost your right to see it." Her hand went to her throat, but he shook his head.

"It pleases me," he said, "to be made a confidant, but I take the will for the deed. If there is anything more you might wish that I should say, imagine that I have said it—congratulations, good wishes, and that sort of thing; you understand."

He had reached the door, but again she called him back. She paused, with her hand on the piano, and struggled for her words. "Carty," she said, "once I told you that it was all off, that I never could marry you—that I should never marry any one. You're glad now, aren't you? You see it is best?"

"Would it make you happier if I said so?" he replied.

"I want to know the truth," she said.

"I am afraid the truth would only hurt you," he answered.

"I want the truth," she said again.

"It is soon told," he said; "there is nothing new to tell."

"What do you mean?" she whispered.

"Isn't it clear?" he answered. "Do you want to bring up the past?"

"You love me?" she asked. He could hardly hear, her voice trembled so.

He made no answer, but bowed his head.

- 46 -

When she saw, she turned, and, throwing her arms along the piano, hid her face, and in a moment he heard her crying softly.

He paused uncertainly, then he went to her. "Sally," he said.

She lifted her head. She was crying still, but with a great light of happiness in her face. "There is no Captain Wynford," she sobbed. "If you had looked in the locket—" A laugh flashed in her eyes.

And then he understood.

They were standing close together in the mullioned window where three hundred years before a man standing on the lawn outside had scrawled with a diamond on one of the little panes:

If woman seen thro' crystal did appere

One half so loving as her face is fair

And a woman standing inside had written the answering lines:

Were woman seen thro', as the crystal pane,

Then some might ask, nor long time ask in ——

The rhyme word was indicated by a dash, but neither the tracings of those dead hands, nor the ancient lawns, nor the oaks that had been witness, did these two see. When many things had been said, she opened the locket.

"You must look now."

"I will," he said. As he looked, his eyes grew misty. "Both of us?" he whispered.

"Both of you!" she answered. And it was so, for in the corner of the picture was Penwiper.

IV
THE CASE OF THE EVANSTONS

Carty Carteret went into the club one June afternoon with the expectation of finding Braybrooke there, and selling him a horse. Braybrooke was not in the club, but Mr. Carteret came upon three men sitting in the bow-window. They had their backs to the avenue, and were apparently absorbed in discussion. As he approached, Van Cortlandt, who was speaking, glanced up and stopped. At the same moment Mr. Carteret drew back. They were not men with whom he cared to assume the familiarity of intrusion.

"Sit down, Carty," said Shaw. Mr. Carteret hesitated, and Shaw rose and drew another chair into the circle. "Go on with the story," he said to Van Cortlandt.

"I dare say Carty has heard it," observed Van Cortlandt, apologetically, as he was about to resume his narrative; "he's a pal of Ned's."

Mr. Carteret looked at him inquiringly.

"I was telling them about the Evanston affair," said Van Cortlandt.

Mr. Carteret opened his cigarette-case and took out a cigarette. "What is the Evanston affair?" he said shortly. He was more interested than he cared to show.

"They've caught Ned Palfrey," said Crowninshield, with a laugh. Mr. Carteret turned to Van Cortlandt. "What do you mean?" he said.

"It's a fact," said Van Cortlandt. "It seems that last Thursday Frank Evanston came home unexpectedly, and found Ned there. Exactly what happened no one knows, but the story is that the gardener and a footman threw Neddie out of the house and into the fountain." Mr. Carteret threw away his cigarette, and straightened himself in his chair.

"And they say," observed Crowninshield, "that his last words were, 'Come on in, Frank; the water's fine.'" There was a general laugh in which Mr. Carteret did not join.

"Is that all?" he asked.

"That's the cream of it," replied Van Cortlandt. "The rest is purely conventional—separation and divorce proceedings."

"That's an interesting story," said Mr. Carteret, calmly, "but untrue."

"How do you know?" said Shaw.

"Because," he answered, "on Thursday, Ned Palfrey was at my house in the country."

"Dates are immaterial," said Crowninshield. "Very likely it was Wednesday or Friday."

"I say," said Van Cortlandt, "I'll bet you even, Crowny, it was Friday as against Wednesday."

"I'll take that," said Crowninshield; "but how shall we settle it?"

"Leave it to Ned," said Van Cortlandt. There was another laugh.

"In the second place," continued Mr. Carteret, disregarding the interruption, "I know for a fact that last evening the Evanstons were still living together in the country."

"Well, I know there is going to be a divorce," said Van Cortlandt. "I got that from a member of Emerson Whittlesea's firm, and he's Evanston's lawyer."

"A lawyer who would tell a thing like that ought to be disbarred," said Mr. Carteret. "If I could find out who it is, I should try to have it done."

"Why?" said Crowninshield.

"Because the three people concerned in the story that he has furnished a foundation for, are my friends."

"So they are his," said Van Cortlandt; "so they are ours. That's what makes it interesting. What's the use of friends," he went on, "if you can't enjoy their domestic difficulties?"

Mr. Carteret rose. "That is a matter of opinion," he said stiffly.

"Well," retorted Van Cortlandt, "there's nothing one can do about it."

"Have you ever tried?" said Mr. Carteret.

"Have you?" said Van Cortlandt.

Mr. Carteret made no reply. He turned on his heel and left the room. Half-suppressed laughter followed him into the hall, and he went on to the billiard room to "cool out," as he expressed it. He was very angry. He paced several times to and fro beside the pool-table; then, with a sudden determination, he walked rapidly out of the club and got into his motor.

"Go to Mr. Palfrey's," he said to the chauffeur. "Hurry." A few blocks up the avenue the car drew up to the curb, and he got out. He crossed the sidewalk, and disappeared into the great apartment house where Palfrey had his rooms. Half an hour later he came out and hurriedly entered the car. He motioned to the chauffeur to change places. "I'll drive," he said. "How is your gasolene?"

"The tank's full, sir," said the man.

"Good," he answered.

He started the car, and began to thread his way up the avenue. At 59th street the clock on the dash-board said ten minutes to six.

He turned into the Park and ran through the avenues at a speed which made arrest imminent, yet he escaped. The Park was a miracle of flowering things, of elms feathering into leaf, of blossom fragrances, of robins at their sunset singing; but Mr. Carteret was unaware of it all. At ten minutes past six he was in the open country. Here he opened the throttle and advanced the spark. He called upon the great machine for speed, and the great machine lifted its shrill roar and gave generously. The clock and the trembling finger of the speedometer showed that many of the miles and minutes passed together. At ten minutes of seven he turned into the gateway of a great country-place, and a few moments later came upon its master on the west terrace. Evanston greeted him pleasantly, but was evidently surprised to see him.

"Did you motor down?" he asked.

"Yes," said Mr. Carteret; "sixty minutes from 59th street."

Evanston gave a low exclamation.

"It wasn't difficult," said Mr. Carteret, "the road's very good." An awkward silence followed, which both men felt.

"Lovely view," said Mr. Carteret, looking off across the lake toward the sunset. Then there was another silence.

Evanston broke it. "Have you still got that horse that you wanted to sell me?"

"I think so," said Mr. Carteret; "but I'm not trading horses this afternoon." His voice changed and he looked at Evanston.

"Frank," he said, "can you keep your temper?"

"I've had some practice," said Evanston. "Why?"

"Because," said Mr. Carteret, "I'm going to irritate you. I'm going to butt in. I'm going to mix up in a matter that is none of my business. If you want to knock me down, I sha'n't like it, but I sha'n't resent it."

Evanston looked at him suspiciously. "What do you mean?" he said.

"From what I've heard," said Mr. Carteret, "your private affairs are in a tangle."

"So you've heard?" said Evanston.

- 50 -

"Yes, I have heard a good many things which are probably not so. I want to know the facts."

Somewhat to his surprise, Evanston made no show of resentment. "The facts are simple," he said. "I'm tired of this thing, and I'm going to put an end to it."

"I've heard that," said Mr. Carteret; "but if you don't mind telling me, I'd like to know why. I like you, Frank," he added; "I like your wife; I like your children—I don't want to see you bust up."

"You are very good, Carty," said Evanston, "but nothing can be done about it. It's a long story, with rights and wrongs on both sides; but at the beginning it was my fault, and I am ready to pay for it."

"What do you mean by 'your fault at the beginning'?" asked Mr. Carteret.

"I married her," said Evanston.

"Well, didn't you want to?" asked Mr. Carteret.

"I wanted to too much," said Evanston; "that was the trouble."

Mr. Carteret looked puzzled. "I don't think I understand," he said. From his somewhat objective point of view the more complex personality of Evanston was baffling.

"It was this way, Carty," Evanston went on. "Her mother—you know her mother?"

Mr. Carteret nodded. "Always for the stuff," he observed.

"Exactly," said Evanston. "Well, to put it bluntly, she made the match."

"But I thought you were rather keen about her."

"So I was," said Evanston; "but Edith wasn't keen about me. The mother forced her into it, and I was foolish enough to believe that if she married me, she would care for me. The fact was," he added, "I was walking on air, with my head in a dream."

"I understand," said Mr. Carteret.

"Well, we were married," continued Evanston, "and then suddenly out of a blue sky came the panic and the T. & B. failure, and I was flat broke and a defaulter."

"Defaulter!" said Mr. Carteret.

"Defaulter as to my side of the matrimonial bargain, which was to provide the establishment," said Evanston. "The realization of this fact was sudden and painful."

"Sudden? How do you mean sudden?" asked Mr. Carteret.

"Something happened," said Evanston, "that opened my eyes."

"Do you mean the loss of your money?"

"No," said Evanston, "you know the money end of it came out all right. My uncle died, and I inherited more than I had lost; but I had already learned how much and how little money could do. And so things drifted along, and now the only course open seems to be to call it all off." Evanston was silent.

"Is that all?" asked Mr. Carteret.

"Yes," replied the other.

"Frank," said Mr. Carteret, "you have told me everything but the facts. Don't interrupt," he went on, as Evanston made a gesture of protest. "The essence of the matter is this—you think that your wife is in love with Ned Palfrey; you believe Palfrey in love with her, and you are jealous of him."

"I don't see the need of going into that," said Evanston. "There is no scandal. I trust my wife and I trust Palfrey."

"The need of going into it," said Mr. Carteret, "is to set you right on two points. First, your wife doesn't care for Palfrey except as a friend, and if I am any judge of what is going on in a woman's mind, she cares more about you than you will allow her to show you. Secondly, except as a friend, Palfrey doesn't care for your wife."

"Carty," said Evanston, "you are wasting your time and mine. I know that a man is foolish to be jealous of any other man, and I know that Ned Palfrey is all right. I'm sorry for Palfrey. He has as much cause for resentment against me as I have against him. If it hadn't been for me he would have married her. If he marries her later on, I shall have no feeling about it. But I can't stand the situation as it is, and I don't care to have you tell me there is nothing in it."

"You have no proof," said Carteret, "that there is anything in it."

"No proof?" said Evanston. He smiled bitterly. "Only the proof of my eyes."

Carteret threw away his cigarette. "The proof of your eyes!" he said.

Evanston nodded. "Perhaps you remember," he went on, "that just after the crash I disappeared for a week."

"Yes," said Carteret; "it was two years ago, just before Christmas."

"People said that I was hiding from my creditors; that I had gone to Australia; and some that I had killed myself."

"That was what Edith believed," said Mr. Carteret. "It nearly killed her."

Evanston laughed scornfully. "Women don't die of such things," he said. "Well, to go on, it happened that the day I disappeared, Palfrey called upon my wife. We were at the house in 70th street then." He paused uneasily, and Mr. Carteret began to wonder. "I came up-town late in the afternoon," he continued, "and let myself in with a key. I heard voices in the drawing-room and went down the hall. The curtains in the drawing-room doorway had fallen apart, and I looked in. Palfrey was there. They were standing by the fireplace and had dropped their voices so that I couldn't make out what they were saying, but I saw him take a step toward her, and then he took her hand." Evanston stopped. "And then," he added, "the sawdust dropped out of my doll."

"What happened?" asked Mr. Carteret.

"He kissed her," said Evanston.

Mr. Carteret started inwardly. Then an illumination came to him. "No," he said; "she kissed him."

"As a gentleman," said Evanston, "I would rather put it the other way."

"As a gentleman," said Mr. Carteret, "you must put it the way it was."

"Does it make any difference?" asked Evanston.

"The difference between right and wrong," said Mr. Carteret. "Listen to me. You knew, I suppose, that Palfrey wanted to marry Edith's sister Louise."

A look of wonder came into Evanston's face. "No," he said.

"Well," said Mr. Carteret, "he did. I know it, and when you saw him at their house and thought he was after Edith, you were barking up the wrong tree."

Evanston had risen, and was listening apprehensively. His face had grown white.

"What has this to do with the case?" he demanded.

"The afternoon that you speak of," Mr. Carteret went on, "Louise told Palfrey that she was going to marry Witherbee. With that piece of news he went to your house, to the woman who had been his friend and confidante— your wife. He was a good deal cut up, and when he said good-by—you know he sailed for Europe the next day—I presume she was sorry for him, and, being a generous woman, an impulsive woman, she showed her sympathy; she kissed him as you would kiss a broken-hearted child."

Evanston made a strange gesture, as if to put away by a physical action the thoughts that were forcing themselves into his mind. "No," he said huskily; "it isn't true, it can't be true."

"Do you think I would come to you with a lie?" said Mr. Carteret.

"But you weren't there," said Evanston. "How do you know?"

"Neither were you," said Mr. Carteret. "Why didn't you go in like a man and find out your mistake?"

For a time Evanston made no answer. Then his voice sank to a whisper. "I was afraid," he said. "If I had gone in I was out of my head." He dropped into his chair again, and turned his face away. His body shook convulsively, but he made no sound. Carteret stepped awkwardly to the terrace balustrade and stood gazing at the sunset. The silence lasted for several minutes. Then Evanston spoke; his voice was still uncertain. He rose and walked unsteadily toward the balustrade.

"Carty," he said, "I believe you. What shall I do? It's awful," he muttered; "it's awful."

"It's awfully lucky," said Mr. Carteret, "that we have straightened things out."

Evanston shook his head wearily. "But we haven't," he said; "we can't. It's too late."

"Look here," said Mr. Carteret, impatiently, "don't be an ass."

"But don't you understand," said Evanston. "If what you say is true,—and I believe you,—then I have acted—" he stopped and thought for the right words, but they did not come. "I left her that afternoon without a word. A week later, without explanation, I came back, and for two years I have treated her—God knows how I have treated her!" he murmured. "If she did care for me at the first," he went on, "if she cared for me after the failure, the end of it must have come when I went away and came back as I did. And now to put an obstacle in the way of her freedom, to try to buy her again, would be the act of a blackguard."

"But suppose she loves you?" said Mr. Carteret.

"That," said Evanston, "is impossible."

"It ought to be impossible," said Mr. Carteret. "If she poisoned you any jury would acquit her; but, fortunately for us, women are not logical."

"No," said Evanston again; "it is impossible."

"That is your view of it," said Mr. Carteret. "Would anything convince you that you are wrong?"

Evanston was silent a moment. Then he smiled bitterly. "If the thoughts she had about me in those days," he began,—"in those days after I had come home,—if they could come back like ghosts, and should tell me that all that time she cared for me, in spite of what I was and did—" He paused.

"Then of course it is impossible," said Mr. Carteret, dryly.

He turned away toward the sunset again and looked at his watch. It was a quarter past seven. In the last twenty-five minutes his hopes had flown high and fallen dead. Evanston's point of view was beyond his comprehension. He felt that the man was mad, and that he had come upon a fool's errand.

He turned back toward Evanston. "I must be going," he said. At that moment a servant came from the house and approached them.

"Mr. Whitehouse is on the telephone, sir," the man said to Evanston. "He says his cook has been taken suddenly ill, and may he come to dine to-night and bring Professor Blake."

Evanston looked helplessly at Mr. Carteret. "That's odd," he said, "isn't it?"

"He evidently hasn't heard," said Mr. Carteret.

"Evidently," said Evanston. "But why shouldn't he come?" he added. He turned to the man. "Tell Mr. Whitehouse that Mrs. Evanston and myself will be glad to have him and Professor Blake." The man bowed and went back to the house.

"It's better that way," continued Evanston. "We'll have a party. I don't know who Blake is; but Whittlesea's coming down, and you'll stay."

"I can't; I have no clothes," said Mr. Carteret.

"That doesn't matter," said Evanston.

"No," said Mr. Carteret, "I must go. I'm of no use here."

"Don't say that," said Evanston. He held out his hand. "Carty, you are the only human being that understands or wants to understand."

"Then," said Mr. Carteret, "I'll stay."

It was nine o'clock, and they had finished dinner. From the dining-room the men went to the library to smoke, and Whitehouse's friend, the Professor, began to talk. He was an Orientalist, and had recently discovered a buried city on the plateau of Iran. Mr. Carteret was not interested in buried cities, so he smoked and occupied himself with his own thoughts. From the distant part of the house came the music of a piano. He knew that it was Edith playing in the drawing-room. It occurred to him that it would be pleasant to go out upon the terrace and listen to the music. He was meditating the execution of this project when he saw Whittlesea slip out; the same idea had occurred to the lawyer.

Mr. Carteret watched him go with chagrin, but he felt that it would be rude for him to follow, so he sat where he was, and bore up under the buried city. The talk went on until suddenly the cathedral clock in the hallway began to strike in muffled arpeggios. Whitehouse started up and looked at his watch.

"It's half-past nine," he said to the Professor. "If you really must take the night train, we ought to be starting."

"I'll ring," said Evanston, "and have somebody order your trap."

"Thank you," said Whitehouse, "I would rather order it myself; I want to speak to my man. I know where the stable telephone is." He went out.

"I am sorry you have to go," said Evanston to the Professor.

"So am I," the Professor replied. "This has been a most delightful evening."

Just then Whitehouse put his head in the door. "The stable telephone is out of order," he said, "I'll have to ask you to send some one, after all."

"The telephone's all right," replied Evanston; "the trouble is, you don't know how to use it." He rose, and joining Whitehouse, left the room.

As he went out, the Professor started to rise, but something held him, and he sat back awkwardly. His sleeve-link had caught in the cord of the cushion on which his arm had been resting. He stooped to disentangle it, and turning the cushion over, his eyes rested on a curious pattern worked in gold. He gave a low exclamation of surprise, and carried the cushion into the lamplight.

"Anything the matter?" inquired Mr. Carteret. To him the Professor was rather curious than human, but he felt that it was civil to show an interest in him.

"There's a verse," replied the Professor, "embroidered in Persian characters on this cushion. It's the work of a poet little known in Europe. It's very extraordinary to find it here."

"Really," said Mr. Carteret, suppressing a yawn.

"I'll make you a translation of it," said the Professor.

"I should be pleased," said Mr. Carteret.

There was a silence, during which the Professor wrote on a stray sheet of paper, and Mr. Carteret speculated on the chance of his horse Balloonist in the Broadway steeplechase. The Professor was handing the slip of paper to Mr. Carteret when Whitehouse and Evanston came hurriedly into the room.

"I'm afraid you'll have to hurry," said Whitehouse. "We have very little time."

"All right," said the Professor; "but I must say good-by to Mrs. Evanston." He nodded a good-night to Mr. Carteret, and went out of the room, followed by Evanston and Whitehouse.

Mr. Carteret heard the music stop in the drawing-room, and he knew that the Professor was taking his leave. He heard it begin again, and he knew that the guests had gone.

"I must go myself," he thought. "Evanston wants to talk with Whittlesea."

He was about to rise when he glanced idly at the sheet of paper which the Professor had given him. Mr. Carteret was not fond of poetry. He considered it a branch of knowledge which concerned only women and literary persons. But the words of the translation that he held in his hand he read a first time, then a second time, then a third time.

He rose, with a startled sense of being on the brink of discovery, and then Evanston came in.

"You are not going," said Evanston.

"No," said Mr. Carteret, vaguely. "Frank," he went on, "do you know anything about that sofa pillow?"

"What sofa pillow?" asked Evanston.

Mr. Carteret took the cushion with the strange embroidery, and held it in the lamplight.

"That?" said Evanston—"Edith gave me that."

"When?" asked Mr. Carteret.

"It was a Christmas present," said Evanston—"the Christmas after the failure."

"After you came back?"

Evanston nodded.

"Do you know where she got it?" asked Mr. Carteret. "I mean the embroidery."

"She worked it," said Evanston.

"But," said Mr. Carteret, "it's Persian."

"Very likely she got the design from her uncle," said Evanston. "She used to be a great deal with him. You know he was Wyeth, the Orientalist. But what is all this about? Why are you interested in this sofa pillow?"

Mr. Carteret gazed searchingly at Evanston. "The design," he said, "that is embroidered is a verse."

Evanston looked at him uncomprehendingly. "Well," he said, "what of it?"

"I want you to ask Edith what it is," said Mr. Carteret.

"Why?" said Evanston.

"Don't ask why. Do it."

"What use can there be in calling up the past?" said Evanston. "It can only be painful to both of us."

"Never mind," said Mr. Carteret; "do it as a favor to me."

"I think you will have to excuse me, Carty," said Evanston, somewhat stiffly.

Mr. Carteret moved to the wall and rang the bell. Neither man spoke until the servant appeared. "Please say to Mrs. Evanston," said Mr. Carteret, "that Mr. Evanston and Mr. Carteret wish very much that she would come to the library." As the man left the room, Evanston came forward.

"What does this mean?" he demanded.

"My meaning ought to be plain," said Mr. Carteret. "I intend to have you ask your wife what is on that cushion." There was something in his tone, in the look in his eyes, which made Evanston's protest melt away, then transfixed him, then made him whiten and tremble.

Presently they heard the rustle of a woman's dress in the hallway. "Do you understand?" said Mr. Carteret, quickly. "You must ask her. You must force it out of her. If she refuses to tell you, you must choke it out of her. The ghosts have come back!" Then he hurriedly crossed the room to the French window that opened upon the terrace. As he reached the window, Edith stood in the doorway.

"Do you want me?" she asked.

"Frank wants you," he answered, and stepped out blindly into the night. He groped his way across the terrace, and from the terrace went on to the lawn. Overhead the stars looked down and studded the lake with innumerable lights. The night insects were singing. The fireflies glimmered in the shrubbery. The perfume from the syringa thicket was heavy on the still air. Ordinarily these things did not appeal strongly to Mr. Carteret; but to-night they thrilled him. A few steps across the grass and he stopped and looked back. The house was silent. From the library windows the lamplight streamed out upon the terrace lawn. He turned away again and stood listening to the night things—the measured chorus of the frogs in the distant marsh, the whippoorwill that was calling in the darkness on the point. Then he resumed his progress across the lawns. Suddenly he came upon a figure in the darkness, and started.

"Has that fellow gone?" It was Whittlesea's voice.

"Yes," said Mr. Carteret.

"Then I must go back," said the lawyer. "Carteret," he went on, "this is wretched business. One would think that, in a spot like this, on such a night, people ought to be happy."

"You are right," said Mr. Carteret. "Whittlesea," he added, "come along but don't speak." He slipped his arm through the lawyer's and guided their steps back toward the terrace. They mounted it and stealthily approached the library window. From the darkness they could see into the lighted room, and not be seen. The lawyer gave a low exclamation, and drew his arm away.

Evanston and his wife were sitting side by side upon the couch. His arm was about her, and his face was bent close to hers. They made no sound, but her body shook a little, and trembled as if she were weeping silently. The two men parted in the darkness, Mr. Carteret retreating back across the terrace.

Evanston and his wife were sitting side by side upon the couch

The fireflies still were glimmering in the syringa-bushes, the night voices still were chorusing, but Mr. Carteret was unaware of them. He looked vaguely into the heavens. The Milky Way glimmered from horizon to horizon.

"'Has the singing nightingale a thought of the grainfields?'"

he began to murmur.

"'If I love you, oh, my beloved, what are poverty or riches?'"

It was the verse upon the cushion.
He stumbled over a croquet ball in the darkness and brought his eyes down from the heavens.
"Carteret, you're an ass," he muttered. He fumbled for his pocket handkerchief and blew his nose. Then wandered on across the lawn till he came to the path that led to the stables, where his motor was waiting. Here he stopped and looked back at the house. The lamplight was still streaming from the library windows, and the silence, save for the night things, was still unbroken. For perhaps a minute he stood and gazed; then he turned and went down the pathway.

V
THE MATTER OF A MASHIE

Cutting had been taken into the firm, to the disgust of the junior partners. They agreed that he would never amount to much, being given over to sports and unprofitable ways of life.

It came about as a result of Cutting getting himself engaged. There was no excuse for his getting himself engaged. He was poor, and She was poor, and they both had rich friends and expensive ideas of life. But, as sometimes happens in such cases, Providence was fairly shocked into making unexpected arrangements.

Cutting's uncle was the head of the firm. Said he: "I am going to give you six months' trial. If you are not satisfactory you will have to get out. Good morning."

The elder Cutting was a great lawyer. As a man he was a gruff-spoken old person, a worshiper of discipline, and continuously ashamed of his kind-hearted impulses. For forty-five years he had reached his office at nine o'clock in the morning, and had remained there till six at night. After that he went to the club and took his exercise at a whist-table. He considered the new out-of-door habits of professional men a scandal.

The junior partners had grown up in this school of thought, and as a matter of course they disapproved of Mr. Richard Cutting. It was unfortunate that Mr. Cutting cared little whether they disapproved or not. It was also imprudent; for the junior partners not unnaturally had it in mind to make his connection with the firm end with his six months' probation.

The previous week a crisis had been reached. Cutting was away two entire days for a Long Island golf tournament. The junior partners conferred with the senior partner, and there was a very complete unpleasantness.

"I shall be forced to terminate our arrangement unless I hear better reports of you from my associates," said the elder Cutting, in conclusion. He believed it his duty to say this; he was also honestly irritated.

The junior partners were gratified; they considered that they had settled the younger Cutting.

It was a muggy September morning, and the office force was hot and irritable. Something unusual and disturbing was in the air. The junior partners were consulting anxiously in the big general room where most of the clerks worked, and where the younger Cutting had his desk. The younger Cutting had not yet appeared. He came in as the clock was pointing to twelve minutes past ten. The junior partners glanced up at the clock, and went on again in animated undertones.

Cutting opened his desk, sat down, and unfolded his newspaper. He was a beautiful, clean-looking youth with an air of calm and deliberation. He regarded the junior partners with composure, and began to read.

"No," Mr. Bruce was saying; "it is too late to do anything about it now. The case is on to-day's calendar, and will be called the first thing after lunch. Our witnesses haven't been notified or subpœnaed, and the law hasn't been looked up."

Smith shook his head sourly. "The old man is getting more absent-minded every year," he said. "We can't trust him to look after his business any longer. The managing clerk gave him a week's notice, and told him about it again yesterday. You think there is no chance of getting more time?"

Bruce looked at his colleague with contempt. "*You* might," he said sarcastically; "*I* can't."

"Oh, I'll take your word for it," said Smith. "I don't want to tackle Heminway."

Bruce laughed dryly. "The case has been put over for us I don't know how many times already," he said. "I don't blame Heminway. He gave us ample notice that he couldn't do it again."

"That's true," said Smith.

Reed *vs.* Hawkins, the case in question, was a litigation of small financial importance, about which the senior Cutting had formed a novel and ingenious theory of defense. Instead of turning it over to the younger men, he kept it as a legal recreation. But he never got to it. It was his Carcassonne.

The day of trial would come, and he would smile blandly, and remark: "True! That has slipped my mind completely. Bruce, kindly send over to Heminway and ask him to put it over the term. I want to try that case myself. A very interesting point of law, Bruce, very interesting."

The last time this had happened, the great Mr. Heminway observed that professional etiquette had been overtaxed, and that the Reed case must go on. People who knew Mr. Heminway did not waste their breath urging him to change his mind.

Messrs. Bruce and Smith considered the situation for a time in silence.

"Well," said Smith, at last, "it's bad for the firm to let a judgment be taken against us by default, but I don't see anything else to do."

At this moment the elder Cutting emerged from his private office with his hat on. Obviously he was in a hurry, but he paused as he came through.

"Have you attended to that Reed matter?" he asked.

"There's nothing to do but let it go by default," said Bruce.

Mr. Cutting stopped. "Get more time!" he said sharply.

"I can't," said Bruce. "Heminway has put his foot down. No one can make him change his mind now."

"Stuff!" said Mr. Cutting. "Dick, go over and tell Heminway I want that Reed case put over the term." And he went out.

Cutting finished the Gravesend races, laid the paper on his desk, scribbled a stipulation, and leisurely departed.

As the door closed, the junior partners looked at each other and smiled. Then said Smith, "I wish I could be there and see it."

Bruce chuckled. He could imagine the scene tolerably well. "It will do him a lot of good," he said. Then he added: "Don't you think I had better write personally to Hawkins and explain matters? Of course we shall have to pay the costs."

"Yes," said Smith; "it's better to explain at once. It's a piece of bad business."

The younger Cutting announced himself as Mr. Cutting, of Cutting, Bruce & Smith. That was a name which carried weight, and the office boy jumped up and looked at him curiously, for he took him for *the* Mr. Cutting. Then he led him down a private passage into the inner and holy place of the great Mr. Heminway.

"He'll be back in a moment, sir," said the boy. "He's stepped into Mr. Anson's office." Mr. Anson was the junior partner.

The door into the waiting-room was ajar about an inch. Cutting peeped through it, and saw the people who wished to consult the great lawyer. He knew some of them. There was a banker who had recently thrown Wall street into confusion by buying two railroads in one day. There were others equally well known, and a woman whose income was a theme for the Sunday newspapers. Cutting watched them stewing and fidgeting with an unlovely satisfaction. It was unusual for such persons to wait for anybody.

He discovered that by walking briskly toward the door he could make them start and eye one another suspiciously, like men in a barber-shop at the call of "Next!" When this entertainment palled, he played with his hat. Still the great man did not come, and presently Cutting took a tour of inspection about the room. As he reached the lawyer's desk, a golf-club caught his eye, and he stopped. It was a strangely weighted, mammoth mashie. He picked it up and swung it.

"What an extraordinary thing!" he muttered. "It weighs a pound." He looked for the maker's name, but the steel head had not been stamped.

He put it back on the desk-top, and was turning away when a row of books caught his eye. Half concealed by a pile of papers was the Badminton golf-book, an American book of rules, a score-book, a work entitled "Hints for Beginners," and a pamphlet of "Golf Don'ts." In the pigeonhole above lay several deeply scarred balls. Cutting laughed.

Just then he heard a step, and turned hastily around. A tall, imposing figure stood in the private doorway—a man of sixty, with a grim, clean-cut face.

"Well?" said Mr. Heminway, questioningly. He had a blunt, aggressive manner that made Cutting feel as if he were about to ask a great favor.

"Well?" he repeated. "I'm very busy. Please tell me what I can do for you."

"My name's Cutting," the young man began—"Richard Cutting, of Cutting, Bruce & Smith."

The great lawyer's face softened, and a friendly light came into his eyes.

"I am glad to know you," he said. "I knew your father. Your uncle and I were classmates. That was a long time ago. Are you the 'R.' Cutting who won the golf tournament down on Long Island last week?"

Cutting nodded.

"Well, well," he exclaimed, "what a remarkable young man you must be! You see," he added, "I've taken it up in a mild way myself. I'm afraid I shall never be able to get really interested, but it's an excuse for keeping out of doors. I wish I had begun it at your age. Every afternoon on the links is so much health stored up for after life. Remember that!"

"They say it *is* wholesome," said Cutting. "I gathered that you played. I saw a mashie on your desk. If you don't think me rude, would you tell me where you got that thing? Or is it some sort of advertisement?"

Mr. Heminway looked surprised. "Advertisement?" he repeated. "Oh, no. That's an idea of my own. You see, I need a heavy club to get distance. I had this made. It weighs fourteen ounces," he went on. "What do you think of it?" He handed the thing over, and watched Cutting's face.

"Do you want my honest opinion?" said Cutting.

The lawyer nodded.

"Then give it away, Mr. Heminway," said the young man, respectfully, "or melt it into rails. You know you can't play *golf* with that."

The lawyer looked puzzled. "What do you mean?" he asked.

"Why, distance isn't a question of weight!" said Cutting. "It's a fact that you get the best distance with the lightest clubs. Most professionals use ladies' cleeks."

The great lawyer looked thoughtful. "Is that so?" he asked. He was trying to account for this doctrine out of his experience. "It seems absurd," he added.

"It's so, though," said Cutting. He heard the banker in the next room cough ominously. He took up his hat.

"Sit down, sit down!" exclaimed the lawyer. "I want to find out about this. I've been doing pretty well, except at the quarry-hole. That beats me. It's only one hundred and twenty-five yards, so that I'm ashamed to use a driver; and with an iron I go in—I go in too often."

"Everybody goes in at times," Cutting remarked encouragingly; "it's a sort of nerve hazard, you know."

"I go in more than '*at times*,'" said the lawyer. "Last Saturday I lost sixteen balls there—and my self-respect. That's too much, isn't it?"

Cutting looked severely away at the portrait of Chief Justice Marshall. "Yes," he said; "that is rather often." The idea of Mr. Heminway profanely filling up the hill quarry with golf-balls appealed to him. "Still," he went on, "you must pardon me, but I don't think it could have been because your clubs were too light."

"Well," demanded the lawyer, "what do I do that's wrong?"

Cutting looked him over critically. "Of course I've never seen you play," he said. "I should judge, though, that you hit too hard, for one thing."

"I suppose I do," said the lawyer. "I get irritated. It appears so simple."

"You see," Cutting continued, "there are three things that you ought always to keep in mind—"

There was a rap on the door, and a clerk put his head in.

"Mr. Pendleton," he began, mentioning the banker's name.

The lawyer waved him out. "I'm busy," he said; "tell him I'll see him directly. Three things?" he repeated, turning to Cutting. "What are they?"

"In the first place," said the young man, "when you swing, you must keep your arms away, and you mustn't draw back with your body. Your head mustn't move from side to side."

The lawyer looked puzzled.

"Fancy a rod running down your head and spine into the ground. Now that makes your neck a sort of pivot to turn on when you swing. It's like this." He took the club and illustrated his idea. "A good way to practise," he added, "is to stand with your back to the sun and watch your shadow. You can tell then if your head moves."

"That's ingenious," observed Mr. Heminway. He looked about the room as if he expected to find the sun in one of the corners. The awnings were down, and only a subdued light filtered in.

"We might manage with an electric light," he suggested. He turned on his desk-lamp, and arranged it on the top of the desk so that it cast its glare on the floor. Then he pulled down the window-shade.

"That's good," said Cutting, "only it's rather weak. Watch the shadow of my head." He began swinging with the mashie.

"I see," said Mr. Heminway; "that's very ingenious."

"It insures an even swing," said Cutting. "Now, the next thing," he went on, "is to come back slowly and not too far. That's the great trick about iron shots especially. You can hardly come back too slowly at first. All the golf-books will tell you that. It's put very well in McPherson's 'Golf Lessons.'"

Mr. Heminway looked over the books on his desk. "I know I bought McPherson," he said. "I think I lent it to Anson. He's insane about the game." He rang his bell, and a boy appeared.

"Tell Mr. Anson that I want McPherson's 'Golf Lessons,'" he said.

"You see," Cutting went on, "you get just as much power and more accuracy." He illustrated the half-swing several times. "A stroke like that, well carried through, will give you a hundred and twenty-five yards. I have a mashie with which I sometimes get a hundred and fifty."

The lawyer stretched out his hand for the club. "That looks simple," he said; "let me try it."

Just then the boy came back with the book and a note. The note was from the banker. "He told me to be sure and have you read it right off," said the boy.

"All right," said Mr. Heminway. He put the note on his desk. "Tell him that I shall be at liberty in a minute."

"I really ought to be going," said Cutting; "you are very busy."

"Sit down," said the lawyer. "I want to get the hang of this swing. That was a pretty good one," he said, after a pause. "Did I do anything wrong?"

"No," said Cutting; "only you came back too fast, and pumped up and down instead of taking it smoothly; and you moved your head. Keep your eyes on your shadow as if it were the golf-ball. That's better," he added.

The next instant there was a heavy chug, and the fourteen-ounce mashie bit the nap off a patch of carpet.

There was a commotion in the anteroom, but Mr. Heminway seemed not to hear it.

"I was keeping my eyes on the shadow that time," he said.

Cutting laughed sympathetically. "I know it's pretty hard. You have to remember about seven different things at once. It's bad for the carpet, though. You ought to have a door-mat. A door-mat is a good thing to practise on. The fiber gives very much the same surface as turf."

Mr. Heminway rang his bell again. "Joseph," he said, "bring the door-mat here. Tell Mr. Lansing to get a new one for the outer office, and leave this one." The boy came back with the mat. The lawyer kicked it into position, and began again. "This *is* better," he observed. "I'll keep it here till I learn."

"That's the only way to do," said Cutting. "Go in to win. If you practise every day with a proper club, you'll get the hang of it in a month or two. But you *must* use a light club."

Mr. Heminway stopped. "A month or two?" he asked.

"Why, yes," said Cutting. "For a large and rather stout man, you are very active. I've no doubt, if you give your mind to it, you can show pretty decent form in a couple of months. You ought to practise with your coat off, though; it binds you."

The lawyer's mouth became grim, but he took off his coat. There was an office rule against shirt-sleeves.

The lawyer's mouth became grim

Here the office boy appeared again, and the great man glared at him.

"Mrs. Carrington," said Joseph. "She says she's got to see you about important business, and she can't wait, and she's going to sail for Europe to-morrow morning."

"Tell Mrs. Carrington," said Mr. Heminway, "that I shall see her as soon as I am at leisure."

The boy withdrew hastily.

The lawyer took his stance by the door-mat again, and began to swing.

Cutting now settled himself in a chair, and lighted a cigarette.

"That's better," he said presently, "much better. You're getting the trick."

Mr. Heminway stopped for a minute, and straightened up. He was beginning to puff. "I think I begin to see how that's done," he said. "It's simple when you get the knack of it. Cutting, come down and stop next Sunday with me in the country, and we'll go over the course. I sha'n't be able to give you much of a game, but there are some fellows down there who can; and I want you to show me how to get over that quarry-hole."

"I should like to very much," said Cutting. He meant this. The girl who was going to be Mrs. Cutting was stopping at the other Heminways', who had the place next.

"The last time I played that quarry-hole," the lawyer went on, "I took twenty-seven for it. And it's all in that swing," he muttered. He crossed over to the rug, and went to work again. "Criticize me now," he said. "How's this?"

Cutting leaned back in his chair.

"Oh, you must carry it through better," he said. "Let your left arm take it right out. You're cramped. You're gripping too tightly. Try it without gripping with your right hand at all. You'll get the idea of the finish. That's better. Now right through with it! Oh, Lord!" he gasped.

There was a crash of glass, then a great thump, and a hubbub of screams and masculine exclamations. The heavy club had slipped from the lawyer's hand and had sailed through the glass door into the middle of the waiting-room.

There was a crash of glass

The great lawyer hurriedly put on his coat. "I suppose I'll have to straighten things out in there," he observed. "But that was the idea, wasn't it—right out!" There was a twinkle in his eye.

He opened the door. In a circle around the fourteen-ounce mashie stood his clients.

"Oh, just a moment," broke in Cutting. "Can't that Reed case go over the term? My uncle wanted me to ask for a postponement."

"Certainly," said the lawyer. "Tell the managing clerk to sign the stipulation. I'll meet you Saturday at the three-ten train." Then he put on his cross-questioning expression. "Ladies and gentlemen," he said calmly, "whom have I the honor of seeing first?"

Who that person was Cutting never knew, because he at once slipped out through the private way, and got his paper signed. Then he went back to his office, crossed over to his desk, and took up the newspaper again. There were the scores of the medal play at Shinnecock, in which he was interested.

Presently Mr. Bruce happened out of his private room, and Mr. Smith coincidently happened out of his.

"By the way, Mr. Cutting," said Bruce, amiably, "how about that Reed matter?"

"It's put over the term," said Cutting, without looking up. "Here's the stipulation. Hello!" he added, half aloud, "here's Broadhead winning at Newport, four up and three to play. That's funny. Did you see that, Bruce? He's been all off his form, too."

"No," said Mr. Bruce.

The junior partners retired with the stipulation, and were closeted together for a long time. It puzzled them. They were impressed, and to each other they admitted it.

Finally Mr. Smith rose and said that he had to go. "Perhaps we have made a mistake," he observed. "There must be something to this boy. He got this." He waved the stipulation.

"We had better give him more of a chance," said Bruce.

And they did. Gradually they began to comprehend him, and then to like him.

As for Cutting, he unbent himself, and got interested in his work. At the end of the six months they spoke well of him, so that he continued on in the firm; and when he was married they sent him a very beautiful etching of "The Angelus."

VI
THE MEDAL OF HONOR STORY

Nature had made Caswell short, swarthy, high cheek-boned, with dark hair and narrow dark eyes, and for ten years he had been sitting at the feet of the Priest of Lake Biwa, dressing as the Japanese dress, leading their life, and thinking as far as an Occidental may their thought. In these ten years the inscrutable expression of the East had begun to dawn in his eyes. His cheek-bones grew more prominent. His nose had begun to flatten. He was a text for those who hold that the soul makes the face. He could also sit upon the floor with his feet tucked under him for indefinite periods, so that it was not strange that among the Japanese he often passed as Nipon Jin (Japanese man).

One May morning he was in the Kin-Ka-Kuji, sitting by the water on the lower balcony of the temple, watching the ancient carp as they slowly wove and interwove among the lily stems, waiting to be fed. He often came to the garden in May because the tourists were apt not to be there then, for they desert Kioto when the summer heat has begun, and it was his habit to come early in the day because the beauty of the place renews itself with each morning's dew and the fragrance of the new flowers, as if in the first hours of the day a woman should be a girl again.

None of Caswell's friends knew what the esoterism of Biwa was or was not; whether the venerable one with the shriveled, monkey-like face had a sweeter communion with the eternal than others, or was a deceiver, for the disciple never wrote or spoke of his experience, but it was a fact that he had acquired the calmness of the East and that was much, for he had his reasons for desiring peace. After his decade of meditation he could regard the hurryings of men, the catching of trains, and the yoke of small annoyances to which society bends its neck, as one inside watches the buzzing of unclean flies against the pane without.

He opened a book of verses by a Japanese poet and gazed across the little, many-islanded lake, whose surface was a sisterhood of silver pools, each framed in the new green of the young lotus pads. The bamboos on the opposite bank glistened faintly as the intermittent touch of an unfelt, unsuspected breeze stroked their plumes. The air was sweet with pine and the pungent aroma of maples in new foliage, and with perfumes from unseen gardens.

To Caswell each year of the past ten, "More weary seemed the sea, weary the oar." Of late the decision had been ripening to shut the door forever upon his old world, and that morning a divine approval of his course seemed to float into his soul upon a tide of peace. He closed his eyes for a time; then he opened them with a fresh thirst for the beauty of the place. Suddenly he started, for he heard a voice. It was a woman's voice, speaking with a cultivated New England intonation, but literal and unsympathetic. His impulse was to flee.

"The temple is called Kin-Ka-Kuji or Roku-onji," said the voice, evidently reading from a guide-book, "from Kin-Ka-Ku, meaning golden pavilion. In thirteen ninety-seven Yoshimitsu retired from the shogunate—"

"Auntie," interrupted another voice, "sha'n't we shut the guide-book? The garden is lovely enough as a garden."

This was a woman's voice, too, but soft and young, with low, resonant tones that brought a thrill to the senses as sometimes comes with the breath of a remembered perfume.

Caswell glanced out of the corner of his eye and saw a party of tourists filing toward the temple on the path along the border of the lake. At the head marched a gray-haired woman with a kind but somewhat aggressive countenance. She carried an open guide-book. At her heels was a fat, squat, shaven-headed Japanese boy, the guide. Behind him there was a girl. He had only an instant's glimpse of her, but he knew that it was the girl that had spoken; lithe, slender, exquisite in white. He looked across the lake again, but he looked without seeing. The garden was full of the sweetness of blue eyes, the softness of fair hair and the loveliness of a girl's smile.

For a moment it was as if the priest of Biwa had never been. His pulses throbbed, a choking seized his throat. Then the habit of years asserted itself. With an effort of will his mind grew calm and the vision faded. Again he saw the lake, the bamboos upon the opposite shore, the carp in the water weeds at his feet.

"What has the circumstance, the external, to do with the abiding me, the eternal?" he murmured. Then he looked again from the corner of his eye toward the tourists.

She had stopped and was standing by the water's edge, gazing across toward the other shore. He saw her mild, wondering eyes animated with the delight of the garden, the broad, low brow above them, the lines of a sweet, firm mouth parted in a smile, the gleam of white teeth, and then behind her, what he had not noticed before, a great-framed youth with tow hair and a frank, kindly face bronzed with a tropical sun. And as the girl gazed across the little lake the youth gazed at the girl.

Caswell brought his eyes back to his book of verses. His philosophy suddenly seemed to have grown more effective. He smiled inwardly, for an Occidental sense of humor slumbered in the ashes of his old self. Then he became grave again. "Am I a thistledown upon the breeze?" he muttered. He repeated one of the mental formulas which the Buddhists of his sect used to compose the mind and open its doors to the all-pervasive soul.

The party of tourists came on and mounted the balcony. They passed him before they noticed him, for he was in the corner at the end. The girl looked at the view and the young man furtively watched the girl, but the older woman spied Caswell sitting on the floor with his feet under him, an open book in his lap, gazing stolidly across the lake. Her curiosity was aroused.

"Who is that?" she said to the fat Japanese boy.

The Japanese boy sucked in his breath and bowed low.

"Yais, sank you," he said laboriously; "he is, what you say, temple man."

"Do you mean a priest?" asked his interrogator.

"Sank you, ah, no, not priest," sucking his breath again. "I sink perhaps priest, some day."

"Be careful, Auntie," suggested the girl, in a low tone. "You know so many of them speak English."

"I haven't said anything to hurt his feelings," she answered. "It's no disgrace to be a priest, for they are not exactly like other heathens. Ask him," she added to the boy, "if he speaks English."

The boy had often seen Caswell, but he did not know what he was or whence, except that he was a friend of one of the priests. He put the question. Caswell muttered something in Japanese without looking up.

"He say he spek no English."

"There," said the aunt, "I knew he couldn't understand."

"*You* speak very well," said the girl to the Japanese boy.

The fat boy doubled over in a bow, sucked his breath, and beamed. "Ah, no! Sank you," he said, "sank you ver' much."

"Ah, yes," said the girl, smilingly. "Where did you learn?"

"At Kioto mission school," he responded.

"So you are going to be a missionary," said the aunt. "How interesting! You are a good boy."

"Sank you," said the boy, "yais, I am temple man boy; some day, perhaps, priest."

"Buddhist priest?" repeated the aunt in surprise.

The boy sucked his breath and bowed.

The young man laughed quietly.

"I think this is rather extraordinary," said the aunt.

"It is rather the rule," said the young man. "The Japanese appreciate our missionary efforts, only they use them in their own way. It is useful to have a temple boy who speaks a little English."

"Well," said the aunt, "it ought to be reported or something. I don't see why the people of America should pay for educating Buddhist priests."

"Neither do the Japanese," replied the young man, "only they accept what they regard as our eccentricities without raising questions."

"The young man seems to be intelligent," thought Caswell.

The aunt made no reply, but stood meditating for a few moments. Then she opened the guide-book, in which she had her finger at the place.

"In the second story, there are paintings by Kano Masanobi. At the top is the golden pavilion. We can give it half an hour. Take off your shoes," she added; "we mustn't waste time."

She leaned against the rail and extended a foot so that the Japanese boy could remove the shoe.

The young man began unlacing his shoes, but Caswell noticed that the girl stood leaning on the rail. Presently she turned to her aunt.

"I think I'll not go in," she said.

The young man stopped unlacing his shoes, and Caswell saw that the girl noticed it.

"But, my dear child," said her aunt, "what an extraordinary idea! You must!"

"No," she said, gently but firmly; "if you will let me, I think I should rather wait here. You take Mr. Williams and show him the pictures and explain them to him."

"But," said her aunt, "I didn't bring you to Japan to sit on a dock and look at the water. You could do that at home."

"Please don't insist," said the girl, appealingly.

"But I must insist," said her aunt. "It's for your own good."

"But you see you don't understand," said the girl, dropping her voice despairingly.

Her aunt approached her. "Are you ill?" she asked. "Is anything the matter?"

The girl put her arms about her aunt's neck and whispered something in her ear.

Only one word reached Caswell, though they were close to him. It was the word "stocking."

The aunt's face immediately grew severe. The girl blushed and looked down.

Caswell almost laughed. He understood. At least he thought he understood. This exquisite creature had a hole in her stocking.

But the big youth remained immovable, like a crouching statue with a shoe-lacing in his fingers.

"It was thoughtless of you not to have taken care—"

"Please!" said the girl, and she put her hand over her aunt's mouth.

"Well, it's your own loss," said the aunt. "I shall write your mother about it. Come, Mr. Williams," she added, "we have no time to waste. You know these paintings are by the old masters of Japan."

The young man hesitated. "I don't think it is civil to leave you," he said, clumsily, to the girl.

"It's her own fault," said the aunt. "You mustn't be sorry for her."

"She is quite right," said the girl, calmly. "You must go in and see the pictures."

The aunt went in and the young man followed without a word. He was embarrassed.

The girl turned to the rail again, and leaning on it gazed down into the water at the carp. She seemed contented to be alone, and to have the young man with her aunt. It surprised Caswell.

A few feet away he was sitting on the floor, with his eyes seemingly on the book in his lap. But the page was a blank. He was stealthily watching the movements of the girl. She had come like a message from a far country—a country, after all, his own—and to him the message was what the first smell of the June clover fields is to the city man when he goes back to the farm of his boyhood.

How long he sat in this way, Caswell could not have told, but suddenly he heard a muffled step on the balcony, and he knew that the youth was coming back. He knew, too, that the girl also had heard the step, for he saw the color deepen in the side of her cheek and throat and in her little ear. But she made no move.

"Simple one that I am," he said to himself. "She knew that he would come."

The youth made a noise as he took his shoes, and the girl turned.

"Where is auntie?" she asked.

"I left her," said the youth, coloring. "I should rather be here."

"It is too bad that you are missing the pictures," she said.

He shook his head.

"Haven't you some biscuits to feed to the fish?" she asked.

"Yes," he said. "The fat boy provided us." He felt in his pocket and handed her several wafers of rice flour.

She broke one of them and let the crumbs fall. "They say these fish are very old," she observed; "hundreds of years, and they come regularly to the balcony to be fed. Think of all the interesting people who have thrown crumbs to them!"

"Can you think of any one as interesting as you?" he said, half playfully.

She made no answer, but continued feeding the carp. "That biggest one," she observed, "looks very wise. I wonder if he remembers what the Shoguns gave him."

"Probably all crumbs are very much alike to him," said the youth.

He finished putting on his shoes and joined her by the rail.

"We ought to take a walk about," he suggested, after a pause. "There are a number of things to see—the Shogun's well, the Shogun's island, and the hill in the distance, the silk hat mountain which he used to have covered with white silk on hot July days so that it would look like snow."

"The mountain is outside the garden," said the girl. "It would be too far to go to it. Anyway," she added, "I don't think I had better leave the balcony. You see, auntie might come down. Where are you going, after you leave Kioto?" she asked, presently.

"I don't know," he answered. "There are two friends of mine in my regiment coming up to get rid of the fever. I may join them and go into the mountains. But I'm so well now that I really have no excuse to stay here much longer."

"I should think that it would be nice to spend a summer in Japan with brother officers whom you knew well," she observed.

"Do you?" he said.

"Yes," she replied. "Wasn't it odd," she continued, after a pause, "that we should meet you out here when we hadn't seen you for a year and a half, and then on the other side of the world?"

"Yes, it was odd," he said, but he smiled a little as if to hint that it was not so very odd, if one knew the inside facts.

"Of course, we had heard how you had been wounded," she went on, slowly, "but we thought you were still in the Philippines."

"I heard in a letter from home," he said, "that you expected to come to Japan, but I didn't know where you were to be."

She looked down at the carp again and crumbled another biscuit for them. "You promised last night," she said, "to tell me how you won the Medal of Honor. Will you tell me now?"

Caswell started in spite of himself and looked at the youth with surprise. "Williams!" he said to himself. "That is so; it *was* a Lieutenant Victor Williams." He knew the story. Every newspaper on the coast of Asia had printed it. "It is strange," he thought. "He is only a boy."

Under the guise of looking into the water, he bent forward intently to listen. He was curious to hear that extraordinary narrative from the young man's own lips.

"It doesn't make much of a story," Williams replied. "The first thing we knew, a lot of *hombres* got around us and cooped us up in a stone church. Bradshaw, my captain, was knocked over in the first firing."

"Killed?" she asked.

"Yes!" he said. "After that—" He stopped because they heard her aunt calling his name from the balcony overhead.

"Yes!" he answered. "What is it?"

"I wondered where you had gone," she called down. "I just missed you."

"He's telling me a story," said the girl, looking up.

"He ought to be seeing these things of Kano Masanobi," her aunt replied.

"You are awfully good to worry about me," he said. "My mind isn't worth it."

She made no reply and went back into the temple.

"Please go on," said the girl.

"Where was I?" he said. "Oh, yes, Bradshaw was hit and we were in the church, and that is about all there was to it. We had to stay there till we were relieved."

"But you were wounded," she said.

"Yes!" he answered. "It came near being serious, but it really was funny."

"What do you mean?" she asked.

"You remember," he said, "the last summer that I was home?"

"Yes."

"Do you remember that I took some snapshots of a lot of you in the sailboat?"

"Yes," she answered. "It was the day when you climbed part way up the mast and took us in the cockpit. You never sent me any of the prints."

"Is that so?" he said. "Well, you see most of them turned out badly, but there was one that I found in my kit when I got out to the Islands, and sometimes I used to carry it about in a card-case." (He put his hand where the left breast-pocket would have been in a khaki blouse.) "In fact, I rather got into the habit of carrying it, as one gets into the habit of carrying a bunch of keys that don't unlock anything, or a pocket piece. Besides, when it was hot up-country, it was refreshing to have a look at the cool lake and all you people in the boat. Well, when I was hit the bullet came through the left breast-pocket."

"And went through the picture?" she said.

"That was the funny part of it," he answered. "When we started on this particular hike—"

"What's that?" she asked.

"They call any expedition or march a hike."

"Go on," she said.

"Well, when we started I took a blouse along, although one generally hikes in a blue shirt like the men." He paused and she looked at him inquiringly. "But you see," he went on, "I wore a soiled blouse and carelessly left the card-case at my quarters in a clean one."

She looked at him with a perplexed expression. "Then the bullet didn't go through the picture?" she said.

"No, that was the joke on the bullet. Instead of having the picture in my pocket what do you suppose I did have?"

She thought for a moment. "A locket," she suggested, "or a prayer-book."

"No," he said, smiling, "a tooth-brush. The bone handle made the bullet glance so that instead of going through, it went around and did nothing worse than scrape a few ribs."

She looked at him wonderingly for a moment and then dropped her eyes.

"Would you like to see it?" he asked.

"The tooth-brush," she queried, "or the bullet?"

"No, the picture," he said, laughing.

"Yes," she answered.

He fumbled in his breast-pocket and brought out a worn leather card-case. He opened it and produced an envelop. From the envelop he took a small, unmounted photograph and handed it to the girl.

She studied it in silence and a smile broke over her face. "Isn't it funny of Agnes?" she asked. "She doesn't seem to have any nose."

"That's so," he said. "Do you make out Ann, next to George in the stern sheets?"

They leaned on the rail and bent over the faded print till their heads almost touched.

"That's Bess next to me in the sweater," she went on, "and there's Winkle."

"Do you remember," he said, "the boom knocked him overboard just before and he would shake himself on your skirt?"

"Dear little dog!" she murmured. "I don't think my head came out very well," she observed, after a pause. "Something must have been the matter with the film or the paper. There's a smudged spot all over it."

"The climate is very damp in the Islands," he said. "Give it back to me."

Their eyes met as she handed the picture back and she dropped hers. Caswell saw the color stealing into the side of her face again.

She moved a step away and gazed down into the water. "That big carp is getting all the crumbs," she said.

He handed her another wafer and replaced the picture in his pocket.

There was a long silence. The girl spoke first.

"But what did they give you the Medal of Honor for?" she said, slowly dropping crumbs to the fish.

"That is a question that has puzzled me before," he answered.

"But you must have done something," she said.

"Well, there wasn't anything to eat or drink in the church," he began, "nor anything in the neighborhood as far as we knew, except cocoanuts, and I was afraid to go out to get them—"

He stopped, for her aunt's voice was calling again from above. They looked up and saw her on the balcony of the third story.

"Mr. Williams," she said, "you *must* come up and see the gold room."

"Please, no," he answered; "I've put on my shoes."

"Yes, you must," she insisted. "I sha'n't come down until you do."

"You had better go," said the girl. "She means what she says."

"I'll be up at once," he called. He took off his shoes and went in.

The girl finished crumbling the wafer to the carp, and watched them for a time as their grotesque mouths mechanically opened and shut upon the sinking flakes. Then she turned her eyes across the lake and embraced the prospect which Caswell had been absorbing when interrupted by her coming. Presently an idea moved her, and from a little bag she produced a gold pencil and a bit of paper and found a smooth place upon the rail. She wrote a few words, took a pin from her dress and fastened the paper to a post as if for a sign to persons coming out of the temple. She glanced quickly up, and seeing no one, slipped away around the end of the balcony.

When she was out of sight, Caswell's eyes went back to his book of verses, but they carried no impressions from the page to his brain. The thoughts which had been aroused were insistent. They possessed him and he sat and battled with them. He was distracted from his reverie by the fluttering of the paper on the pin. A warm breeze had awakened and came in mimic gales which rippled the pools and set the bamboos on the farther bank in a silver shimmer. After the pin had resisted several onslaughts, a stronger air loosed it and sent the paper fluttering into the water.

Almost before it fell Caswell was on his feet. Then he checked himself. "It is not my business," he thought. "Shall I interfere with the course of Fate?" He sat down. Then he rose again. "But perhaps I am the minister of Fate." He leaned over the rail. The paper was slowly sinking, but he read under the clear water, "I am going to walk. Do you want to come?"

The young man's stick was lying on the balcony. He took it and leaning over the rail fished up the wet paper. As he put his hand upon it, he heard a footfall, and turning saw the big lieutenant coming out of the temple. He had turned in time to catch the youth's expression, as he perceived that the girl was not there.

"Oh!" said the youth, awkwardly. He saw that something had happened.

Caswell bowed in the Japanese manner, sucking his breath as if to a superior, and extended the dripping paper with the inscrutable countenance which the East had taught him.

The youth read it at a glance. "Thank you! Thank you, very much!" he said, impulsively; then remembering himself, he repeated his thanks in Japanese: "*Arigato! Arigato!* I understand," he said, in answer to Caswell's gesture toward the water. "The wind blew it in. You were very good." He repeated the Japanese word again and bowed, and Caswell, bowing solemnly, backed off the balcony and left him.

"It was best so," he thought, when he was on the path by the edge of the water.

He had come to the priest's apartments, the little palace where the great Shogun had lived in his retirement, before he was conscious whither his steps were taking him. His thoughts were across eight thousand miles of sea. He looked around him with a start. "Shall I go in?" he said to himself. One of the priests, although of a different sect, was his friend. On the porch, a temple student saluted him. He was known because he often came, not only to talk with his friend, but to study the screens of Kano Tan Yu and Jakuchu, and the marvelous folding screens painted by Korin and Soami, and the kakemonos by those other ancient masters, Cho Densi and Shubun and Eishin.

He took the student's welcome as an omen and slipped off his sandals. He was ushered in and, after saluting his friend, the temple tea was brought and they sat with it between them and discoursed. The temple tea was not as other tea, but superior. It was a powder made of the tenderest of the young leaves of certain choice plants. It possessed the secret flavors of spring, and the property of making the mind glow and the brain crystal clear without racking the nerves.

They talked for a time, but to Caswell it was with an effort. His soul that day had no meeting with his friend, and the priest was aware of it. He produced tobacco and they lit the little pipes and, inhaling a few whiffs, sat in silence.

Presently Caswell turned his head to listen. Through the paper screen which made the partition wall, he heard the girl's voice; then the voice of her aunt. They were entering the room next.

"It is a party of foreigners," observed the priest. "They have doubtless been generous to the boy. Liberal foreigners are sometimes invited to partake of the temple tea. The tea money (*chadai*) goes to the restoration fund."

"Is it so?" said Caswell. He was listening.

"I am afraid that I never could get used to sitting on my feet," said her aunt.

"Poor auntie!" said the girl, and then she laughed, and as she laughed Caswell held his breath. It was a low, sweet, bubbling laugh; the laughter that is compelled by happiness in the heart, just as a fountain bubbles under a pressure of crystal water.

A moment later came the deeper tones of a man's voice, also laughing, and the echo of the same happiness was in them.

Caswell smiled and a mist came into his eyes. He understood. He looked at the old priest, and he too was smiling.

"The young foreign lady has an agreeable voice," observed the priest. "Unlike most."

"Unlike most who travel here," said Caswell, "she is of an honorable family."

"Friends, no doubt, of your honorable family," suggested the priest.

"No," said Caswell. He realized that he did not even know her name. "But I know," he continued. "One may know by the voice and the speech."

"Assuredly, with us," said the priest, "but I had thought that all families in America were equal."

"Yes and no," replied Caswell, absently. He had no mind for explaining the American system then. He was listening, for they were laughing again, although there seemed no reason for laughter in the conversation.

Presently Caswell rose and began his leave-taking, and the priest accompanied him to the porch where he had left his sandals. Beside the sandals they saw three pairs of shoes.

There was a pair of heavy men's walking shoes, a pair of woman's shoes of the type known as "common-sense," and a third pair on which Caswell's eyes rested. These were little Russia leather things, not new but with the workmanship and fine lines of the Oxford Street bootmaker, and they had the air of well-being which comes from proper trees and the care of an expert maid.

"It is a curious custom of the foreigners to make shoes out of leather," observed the priest.

"It is, is it not?" said Caswell, but absently, for through the half-open wall panel he saw the party seated on the matting around the fire-pot which the fat temple boy had just deposited. The young man and the girl were sitting next one another. The aunt was examining a screen. Their backs were turned to him, so that Caswell could look without being seen. Suddenly, as he gazed at the little shoes, an idea came to him and he smiled.

The fat boy was coming out on his way for the tea and cakes, and as he passed Caswell stopped him.

The boy bowed ceremoniously.

"Did you remove the shoes of the honorable young foreign lady?" he inquired.

"Did you remove the shoes of the honorable young foreign lady?"

The boy bowed again and replied that he had indeed been so honored.

"In the foot of the stocking of the young foreign lady," inquired Caswell, "was there not a hole?"

"Not the least hole," replied the fat boy, wonderingly.

"No hole? Are you sure?" said Caswell.

"None," said the boy.

"Thank you, that is all," said Caswell, gravely. He looked at the little shoes again. "Simple one that I am," he murmured.

"Is it true," inquired the priest, "that foreign women wear stockings above their ankles and of colored fabrics?"

Caswell made no reply for a moment. The girl was speaking.

"But you never told me what you did to win your medal," she said.

"It is true," said Caswell, in reply to the priest's question.

"But I should like to know," said the girl.

"I finally got up the courage to go out after the cocoanuts," said the youth, "after I was good and hungry."

"But what else?" said the girl.

"But that was all—on my word," said the youth, and they fell to laughing again.

"It is a curious custom," observed the priest, referring to the stockings.

"It is," said Caswell, politely, "is it not? And now I must depart," he added.

He bowed his farewell. "*Sayonara!*" he said, "*Sayonara!*"

"*Sayonara!*" said the priest, bowing. "You will come soon again?"

Caswell straightened up. "I forgot to tell," he said. "I shall not return soon. I am going to my own country."

"Indeed, is it so? Is it so?" said the priest, gently. He bowed again and wished him the good wishes suitable to such a parting.

"*Sayonara!*" said Caswell. Then he walked toward the wicket gate that led out of the garden.

"He got up the courage to go out after the cocoanuts," he murmured, as he walked away. He quickened his steps, but once he turned and looked back, for he heard their low, rippling laughter again.